Protecting Faith

Protecting Faith

Angie Dewoody Mitchell

CAPTIVATE PRESS

PROTECTING FAITH

Angie Dewoody Mitchell

To:

Jonathan, for understanding my work.

Shanetta, for always encouraging me.

Marilyn for guiding me to follow God's plan.

All glory to God!

Prologue

He wiped the sweat from his brow with one hand; the other held his high-powered binoculars. His concentration was focused across the street at Lydon B Johnson Elementary School on the figure of a woman. She was loaded with boxes and bags.

He was in the window of an apartment across the street from the school. From that vantage point, he could see the front of the building and the parking lot. He hoped that her classroom would be one of those with windows on the front side of the building, making his job easier.

He had lost her in Dallas. His search had taken months, but now he had found her. How she had chosen Tulsa was a mystery. She had no family here, and he didn't think she had any friends in this part of Oklahoma. Fortunately, Faith wasn't good at hiding her tracks. With his resources, he'd been able to pick up her trail.

He could see that this school was in a bad neighborhood. He knew that she needed him. She was just too strong-willed to admit it. It had caused them problems in the past. The world was cold, and he only wanted to shield her from it.

Again, he wondered why she had run. He had given her everything. She didn't need to work. He took care of her. All he ever cared about was making her happy.

He knew he wasn't a saint. But he loved her more than anyone else ever could. He saw past her imperfections. Maybe she'd had trouble understanding how deeply he loved her.

The front door opened, and a man stepped out. The man was tall and built like a brawler. He, on the other hand, was toned and lean. He kept himself in top fighting form.

He didn't like this man at the school. He'd checked and seen that there was a male principal and one male teacher. They were no threat. This man was neither. He was in uniform. Faith had never been unfaithful to him; she loved him too much to stray. However, this man could pose a problem. He needed her to be unprotected. He was the only one who could offer her actual safety.

The presence of a police officer complicated things. But nothing could stop him. He would bring her back. After all, Faith was and always would be his.

Chapter 1

Faith precariously juggled boxes and bags in her arms when she reached the front door of Lyndon B. Johnson Elementary. She carefully swiped the school ID with her picture to get inside. She swiped it. Once. Twice. She swiped a third time, and the door still wasn't unlocked. She took a frustrated breath. The box and the bags were heavier and more awkward than she expected.

For a moment, she thought she felt eyes watching her. Then her fingers tightened on the boxes- Charles couldn't be watching her- he had no idea where she was. Still, she felt the hairs on the back of her neck stand up. She straightened her back and lifted her head high; she needed to get inside. Ever since she left Dallas, she had been vigilant; she didn't need trouble. She needed a fresh, new start.

She said a little prayer that things would be different and that she would be safe. The Oklahoma summer heat was beating down, even this early morning. She could feel the humid waves bearing down on her from above. Then, a slight breeze tickled her face, and Faith smiled; maybe everything would be okay.

She breathed, dropped the boxes and bags weighing down her hands, and banged on the door. No response. Just as she started to bang on the door again, a man wearing a uniform approached.

The man smiled with eyes as vast and blue as the sky. He opened the door. He towered over her petite frame. The smile on his face was warm, and she couldn't help but smile back.

"Thank you. The ID card they gave me at the service center didn't work."

"Happens all the time," the man stepped aside so she could walk through, then grabbed the remaining boxes.

"Officer Ryan Madsen, at your service."

"I'm Faith Rogers. Um…why does an elementary school need a cop?"

"Why does anyone need a cop?" He winked. "For protection. This neighborhood can be rough at times, and a couple of years ago, there was some trouble. The PTA is small but can be mighty. They got the school administration on board, and voila," he waved a hand, "here I am."

Had she gotten herself in over her head? She felt her body tense up from her toes to her hair. She chewed the inside of her cheek with clenched teeth. All she wanted was a peaceful school where she could thrive; the last thing she needed was violence again.

"I didn't know things had gotten this bad," fear and resignation crept into her voice.

"Now there," he said, adjusting the boxes in his arms, "Don't get jittery. I make sure this school is safe. It's my baby."

He winked again. Even though they had just met, she believed him.

"Oooh! Can you smell that?" Faith asked as they walked further down the hall.

"What? I don't stink, do I?"

"No," she smiled, "that new school year smell. It smells like cleaner and fresh floor wax. It always gives me hope for a good year."

"All that from a little Pine-Sol?" he teased.

"It's silly, I know," she smiled.

She was excited about getting another chance to work with kids. At this school, teaching would be fun again. It had to be better than the last few years.

"Thank you for helping me with my boxes! I'm in room seven."

"This is seven." He said, setting the boxes down, "So, you're the new Pre-K teacher."

"That's me. I'm so glad to be here and to be teaching Pre-K again. I like teaching the little ones. They're sweeter and have a lot less attitude."

"I don't envy you that; from what I've seen, it's a lot of crying, wet pants, and untied shoelaces. I'd rather work with the older kids; they get my jokes," he smiled, "By the way, is it Missus or Miss?"

"It's Miss." Her cheeks felt warm. Was she blushing?

"Good to know," Ryan sauntered back down the hall, and she couldn't help but notice the casual grace and authority with which he walked. She had to get a grip. She had just met this man, and he already had her feeling off-kilter. Halfway down the hall, he stopped, "Since your ID is broken, why don't you take your lunch break with me? I could show you around the area, and you'd be able to get back in."

"I don't know," she wasn't sure whom to trust yet, but his smile was kind and friendly, and he was one of the most handsome men she'd ever met.

"If you change your mind, you know where to find me," he gave her puppy dog eyes.

If she was going to work here, she needed to give the staff a chance, "Wait," she stopped him, "Sounds great; what time?" she gulped back a nervous giggle,

"My lunch break is at noon."

"Then I guess I'll see you at noon," she still felt hesitant, but she refused to let fear guide her actions. Besides, he was a cop; she would be safe.

"It's a date."

Faith went into her classroom, a little flustered. What was she thinking? A lunch date? Was he going to expect more from her after this? Or was he just friendly? She felt so paranoid, unable to trust anyone. She wasn't even sure she could trust her own judgment. He could help her, or he could be trouble. Faith offered a quick prayer, "God, give me discernment and help me know whom to trust."

Ryan was so big; he was strong and carried the tubs easily. Charles had used his strength to control her. Could the police officer use his power to help her? Something about him made her feel safer.

She was attracted to him; that wasn't part of the plan. What was she doing? That was the last thing she needed. She was not in the market for a man. Not even one with a smile like that.

So, she shook it off and began unpacking her tubs. Soon, Faith was hot and sweaty from her work. A light sticky film had formed on her skin from the dust off the tubs of supplies, books, and random teacher paraphernalia. She needed a break.

Faith took a deep breath and sat down at the teacher's desk. This was a new place; nothing was here to remind her of Charles. She could leave all those bad memories behind her. This was a fresh start. She tried to convince herself that she would be safe here. She had felt led to come to this school. She knew the safest place was to be where God had put her.

It seemed Officer Ryan roaming the halls was part of God's plan to keep her safe. That thought brought him back to the front of her mind. Right on cue, her stomach growled. She looked at the oversized clock on the wall. It was nearly noon. It's time for her 'date' with the policeman. The handsome policeman. The policeman that she had no good reason to be thinking about romantically.

She'd promised herself not to get involved with another man. She was sure that kind of relationship was not part of the plan for her life. She had made too many mistakes with Charles; she was afraid she had used up her chance for a loving relationship with a man of her own. Her mom had told her that God was a God of second chances, but she wasn't sure she deserved one.

She heard a tapping at her door with a drawling "Knock, knock" to accompany it. There stood the officer as if her thoughts had conjured him. He brushed his large hand through his short brown hair.

"Officer Mason. Is it noon already?" she gave a little wave.

"It's Madsen, but call me Ryan, please."

"Sorry, I'm terrible with names. Good with funny, but terrible with names."

"Are you still interested in lunch? I could show you all the food spots if you are cool with that," he led her through the halls so she wouldn't get lost.

"Um, okay, sounds good. Anything but hotdogs; I had a bad experience." She put her hand to her face. She could still feel the stinging of Charles' slaps. She would never be able to eat a hot dog again. Even the smell took her back to that feeling of helplessness. She quickly and firmly pushed the thoughts from her mind. She had promised herself not to dwell on the past. She only wanted to focus on the present.

As they exited the building, a slight frown crossed his lips, "Ugh,"

Had she upset him in some way? That would be typical. She remembered upsetting Charles… and the consequences. For a moment, she froze. She told herself she was overthinking things; the police officer seemed easygoing.

"What's wrong? I promise I'm not that picky."

"No, not that. I forgot I came in on the motorcycle today," his voice drizzled with disappointment.

"If you don't mind a mess, we can take my car," she said, hoping to salvage the situation, "You'll have to tell me where to go."

"I don't mind a mess, Faith. After all, you're a teacher, and this is the beginning of the school year," he chuckled, "I'm curious you said you were good with funny and not names. What did you mean by that?" Ryan asked after they got into her car.

"Oh, I do comedy for fun and have terrible name recall."

"Funny and forgetful," he chuckled.

"What? Don't I look funny?"

"I wouldn't say that." His laugh was husky and rendered her speechless.

Ryan continued, "We're a friendly bunch at Johnson. Wait till you meet some more of the others. I'll make sure you meet Mandee and Maggie. They'll eat you up. You'll love the faculty here."

"I'm glad. I met a few teachers this summer at the meeting. I was a little worried about the impression I had made. I tend to be a little obnoxious when I first meet people. I talk too much and act like a huge weirdo; I hope I haven't been acting like that. I can't help it."

"Obnoxious? Who in the world ever told you that?" Ryan wondered.

"My um… ex-fiancé told me he was the only one who could see through my obnoxious exterior. But I don't like talking about the past."

"Sorry to bring it up."

"You didn't; I did. How could you know that about me? I can't believe I even said anything about it to you. I usually don't mention things about him- at all."

"I have a way of bringing out the secrets of a pretty girl's heart."

" I don't know about all that, but I have said more than usual. What's your trick?"

"I do it with mirrors," his laugh was throaty.

They drove around looking at fast food places.

"If you don't like fast food, I can show you one of my favorites. Do you like Philly cheese steak?"

"I've never had it."

"Then, we'll go to Steak Stuffers; not many people even know it's here."

The diner was done up in red, white, and blue, just like the flag. She looked at the posted menu, overwhelmed by the many choices.

"What's good?"

"I always get the cheese steak stuffer. It's authentic, but a lot of food."

They went up to the tiny window. A friendly-faced woman took their orders.

She grinned at Ryan, "The usual?"

"Of course, Karrie."

"I'll have the same," she said, then she searched for her wallet in her big, red purse.

"It's on me." Ryan smiled.

"Thanks, but no. I always split the bill. It's better that way."

As they stood there waiting for their food, Faith looked at the muscle in his bicep peeking out of his sleeve, and when their eyes accidentally met, Faith looked away quickly. Ryan just smiled, obviously pleased. He laughed a little bit, and she felt her face heat. She must be red. What was wrong with her? She knew better.

"Sorry if I made you uncomfortable, Faith, but you are cute."

"I just- I mean- I wasn't… it's just that you, um… you know?" she giggled uncomfortably.

"I have no idea what you just said," He laughed a little smugly, "But thank you, I'm flattered,"

Faith burned and avoided his eyes.

"Sorry again, I shouldn't have embarrassed you; it's just… I've been checking you out since you came in the door to the school."

Was he flirting with her? How was she supposed to react? What should she say?

"It's okay, Ryan. I'm just out of practice," she laughed nervously; what was she getting herself into?

By the time their food arrived, Faith was discombobulated. She found herself feeling attracted to Ryan, and that wasn't good. But there was nothing wrong with a date, especially with a guy who smiled like that. Why did he have to be so gorgeous?

"What are you thinking about? You look serious, Faith. What's going on in your head?"

"Nothing, really," she did not want him to know she was still thinking about him.

"What should we talk about while we eat?" he asked.

"I don't know. Tell me about the school and the other teachers. Is there much scuttlebutt, little dramas that go on at Johnson?"

"We have our fair share."

"So, who really runs the place? The principal? The secretary? The custodian? A particular teacher? Hmmm?"

"Dr. Abernathy- we call him Dr. A. He firmly holds the reins. Some say that Ms. Brown, the secretary, is second in command. Keep on her good side if you want anything. She has the keys to the supply closet and guards the Doctor's door. I'm sure she'll like you; I already do."

"Oh," she had no reply.

"My favorite teacher is Maggie Foster. She is one of the most wonderful women alive."

Faith felt a pang of irritation. Why was he flirting shamelessly with her if he cared so much about this woman? Was he some kind of player?

"What's wrong? You've stopped smiling. I like that smile."

"Nothing, I just wanted to hear more about Miss Foster," she knew this was a bad idea.

"Maggie was my mom's best friend- she's my second mom. She is an angel."

"She sounds sweet; I can't wait to meet her." Her smile returned. She felt like an idiot for assuming things about a man she had just met; he could be different.

"Now, Faith, tell me about yourself."

"I don't like to talk about myself."

"I'm interested in knowing more about you. You've got me curious."

"Well, you'll just have to be curious- but remember, it was curiosity that killed the cat." she shivered.

She knew just how dangerous that kind of curiosity could be.

Chapter 2

Ryan was standing at his post by the front doors of the school. He started pacing the width of the foyer. He was trying to escape his thoughts. The first day for the kids always made him think of his mother. She had died. He made himself face the unpleasant truth… she had been killed on the first day, two years ago, on her way home from school. He needed to focus. The first day was always brimming with parents. All the people coming in and out meant he had to keep a closer eye. He stopped pacing and watched the doors. New parents that he didn't know were always a potential threat.

Looking for him, Maggie Foster came down the long hall from the cafeteria.

"Hey, Honey," she said with a wave of her hand.

"What's up, Maggie?" He smiled at the small, heavy-set woman.

"If you want to come over after school for dinner tonight, I've got a roast in the crock pot. Besides, you stood me up on Sunday."

"Sorry about that; I accidentally slept in." he averted his eyes sheepishly.

"It's all right; just make sure you come next Sunday."

"You know you don't have to feed me all the time. I'm a big boy; I can cook for myself."

"I know you can. But since Tony died last year, I've missed having a man around the house."

"Okay, Maggie, I'll come over tonight. You spoil me even more than Mom did."

"I know that this is a hard day for you. It's a hard day for me too. Your mom was my best friend."

"It just hits me hard on the first day. She was so excited and hopeful about the year. I miss that."

"I do, too. You know I love you like you're one of my boys. I'm always here if you need me."

"Love you too," he bent over to hug her.

"By the way, I saw you leaving with the new teacher for lunch last week. Do you want to talk about it?" her eyes were full of concern.

"Not particularly."

"She's pretty. Watch your step. You don't have a great track record with dating teachers."

"I know, I know, Maggie. You don't have to tell me again."

"Honey, I hope you learned your lesson. Have you seen Ashley today?"

"Unfortunately, yes. Ashley was… unpleasant; I wish I'd listened to you."

"Of course you do. I give great advice; you just don't always take it."

"I wish I had before I got involved with Ashley." He groaned.

"Cheer up, Ryan; she might finally be over the whole mess."

"I doubt it. She hates me. She's been trying to turn the other teachers against me."

"Most of them took your side."

"I wish I'd never gotten involved with her. Faith is different, and one lunch doesn't mean anything. Besides, I haven't seen much of her since. She's barely come out of her room, not that I've been checking."

"Just be careful."

"I'm always careful."

He walked down the hall with her toward her classroom, ever alert.

"The invitation still stands if I don't see you before I leave."

"Okay, Maggie, I'll be there."

He ambled to the front doors. He started pacing again as his thoughts went to Faith this time. He could picture her laughing brown eyes as they joked through their lunch.

It was better to think of the future instead of the past. He told himself his future was not tied up to a woman, especially not a teacher. But his thoughts kept straying back to his time with her. He'd had fun as she'd told him funny stories of her teaching experiences. Her joy at the beginning of the new school year had reminded him of his mother.

That lunch date had been a mistake. He'd let her beauty mess with his common sense. He couldn't start dating, especially not a teacher. Definitely not a woman like his mother. He didn't want to open himself up to that kind of pain. A woman like that would want more than he was willing to give.

After his mom had been killed, he shook his head, trying to clear his brain of the uncomfortable thoughts. He couldn't get it off his mind.

After that, he closed himself off from any attachments. That was the only way he knew to avoid that pain again. If you steered clear of relationships, you steered clear of heartaches.

It was all so unfair.

"Why God?" he asked again, expecting no answer.

He'd given up on God, too. His mom had been a strong Christian, and she'd tried to instill her values into him. He'd been one. But after she was killed, he'd turned away from his beliefs. How was he supposed to trust a God who let that tragedy happen? He'd rely on himself, and with his police training, he could care for those around him. But wouldn't let anyone else in his heart.

Ryan restlessly couldn't stand still. His thoughts were churning. He saw Ashley Sheridan come down the hall with a big folder. The last person he wanted to see. She came up to him with malice in her eyes.

"I heard you took that new Pre-K teacher to lunch last week."

"That's none of your business."

"I'm making it my business. Someone has to look out for the new girl."

"I'm not the big bad wolf."

"No, you're worse. You're a wolf in sheepdog's clothing."

"Ashley, surely you have something more productive to do than harass me."

"I'm going to warn her about you."

"Who I eat lunch with is not your concern."

"That woman needs to know that you are nothing but a player."

"I never cheated on you, Ashley."

"Maybe not, but you played me for a fool. I should never have trusted you."

"Ashley, we weren't right for each other. You know that."

"That's because you never gave us a fair chance."

"If you think logically about it, you'd see I'm not your guy."

"You never gave me a chance to find out if we could have something. You're just too afraid to commit."

"I told you at the beginning that I wasn't looking for anything serious."

"You made that clear when we broke up. That is why I'm going to warn her about you."

"Go ahead. Do what you like."

"I've got to go; it's my planning time, and I've got copies to make."

Then she turned on her high heels and marched down the hall to the auxiliary room.

She was so unpleasant. She was going to mess things up with Faith before they started. Maybe that was for the best. The last thing he needed was a woman in his life. He had Maggie, and that was enough.

He had even tried to pull back from Maggie. She had worked with his mom for as long as he could remember. Maggie wouldn't let him pull away from her. So, he worked even harder, building the wall around his heart to keep out everyone else. Ryan would never get hurt again.

His life was safe right now. He didn't have any attachments, except Maggie, and only because she wouldn't let him stay away from her. He was lonely, in any case. Maggie was fantastic, but he wanted something more. He wanted to start dating again, but on his terms. He didn't want to be in love. Love was dangerous.

It was almost lunchtime; he should be preparing for his midday rounds. The transitioning from lunch to recess and back to the classrooms was always a busy time. He kept on alert; his lunch break was right before the Pre-K went to lunch, and then he would be on patrol until the last class was back inside. Last year, the Pre-K teacher had her planning time before the kids' lunch. He would see her hurrying through her lunch as she worked in the teacher's lounge while he took his break. He had observed that the Pre-K teacher usually stayed in the lunchroom with the kids. He wondered if Faith would do the same. He reprimanded himself for thinking about her as he walked to the lounge with his lunch.

Chapter 3

It was the first day of school. She felt her lips tip in a smile. Faith was hopeful that this year was going to be better. All the teachers she'd met had been friendly. Her room was just the way she wanted it. She was incredibly grateful that her new teacher's assistant, Evon Walton, was so much fun and had been such a big help in getting everything ready. They had become friends almost instantly.

Then there was Ryan, the policeman. She couldn't stop thinking about him. They'd not had another lunch date, which made her vaguely disappointed. She tossed her hair as she told herself that she didn't care if she'd scared him away. It would be better that way. But she admitted that having him around the school made her feel safer.

The day began as expected, with lots of tears from the little ones who had never been away from home. By her planning time, she was already exhausted but content. She took her lunch bag into the teacher's lounge and sat down with a sigh. She'd have to use her planning time to eat lunch because she would spend lunch in the cafeteria with her kids. She'd never get a chance to eat; there was always a minor emergency: spilled milk, spilled food, and she'd always had to peel their oranges. Maybe this class would be different, but she doubted it.

"Hard day?" she nearly jumped out of her skin; startled by Ryan's sudden words, she'd thought she was alone. For a tiny second, she had thought it was Charles. He loved scaring her. Ryan was lounging on a chair at the worktable, eating something that looked like leftovers. His eyes were friendly, and his smile was mischievous.

"You startled me."

"Sorry. I wondered how it was going; I'd heard crying all day. It seems one kid hasn't stopped yet."

"Yes, Damiana is her name; she's never been away from her grandmother. I'm ready to drop on my feet. But watch, I'll have her happy to be here by the end of the week."

"You must have the patience of an angel. Doesn't that bawling set you on edge? I'd go out of my mind if I had to listen to it all day.

"It gets better. The first couple of weeks is the hardest."

"Two weeks? I don't know how you do it."

"I like my kiddos; once they get used to being here, they'll be the best. It will be worth it. Their little faces will light up when they see me; it's a great feeling."

"I'm glad to talk to you; you've been so busy getting ready that I didn't get another chance to talk to you. Does Johnson meet your expectations?"

"It's been good so far. Everyone has been friendly; I think this will be a great year," she thought it had to be better than the last three years; she loved teaching and knew she was finally in a safe place with Ryan at the school.

Faith took several bites of her PB&J and a long drink from her water bottle. She could see Ryan eyeing her curiously.

"What? Do I have something on my face?"

"No," he straightened up in his seat. "I was just wondering if you would like to meet up after the kids go home."

"Oh!" she was at a loss for words. "I would like that, but we have a teacher's meeting after school." Could he hear the disappointment in her voice? She didn't want to feel disappointed.

"No worries, maybe another time."

She looked up at the digital clock on the wall. The lunch bell would ring in a few minutes, and she needed to be early to take her kids to the cafeteria.

"It's nearly time to get back to my class," she was reluctant to end the conversation.

"Yes, duty calls. I'll see you on my rounds. Good luck!"

"Thanks."

At the end of the school day, she had her little ones all packed up and in a semblance of a line as she led them to be dismissed. Faith was holding Damiana's hand because she was still crying. They left the building to stand against the outside wall, waiting for the children to be picked up. She felt an uncomfortable pricking on the back of her neck; she was being stared at. She tried to shake it off. She felt suddenly exposed and unsafe. For a frantic second, she scanned the schoolyard, and then her eyes met the policeman's eyes, and he gave her one of his heartwarming smiles. The feeling dissipated. Ryan was here; she was safe. She sent up a quick prayer of thankfulness for Ryan and the safety he provided.

There was something about him that inspired a feeling of well-being. He was muscular and looked like he could handle himself in a fight. He exuded strength and power as he stood in his place, watching over the school like a guardian angel. He caught her eyes with his, and his smile was reassuring. Her fear of Charles abated a little when he was around, and she felt like she could breathe easier. Maybe that is why she wanted to spend time with him.

She flopped down on the bench next to the two kindergarten teachers in the foyer when all her kids had gone home. All three of them exchanged weary glances as they heard one last cry from the last little kindergartener whose parent was late.

"How many criers did you have today?" Faith asked Angel and Kat.

"I had three," sighed Angel, shaking her short caramel hair.

"I only had one, but he never stopped crying," Kat told them, pulling a strand of red hair out of her face.

"Most of mine stopped crying by lunchtime, but Damiana cried till she fell asleep at rest time, then she woke up and cried till her grandma picked her up."

"Ladies, you are heroes." Ryan sauntered to where they sat, "I don't think I could do it."

"The crying usually only lasts a week or two," Kat said.

"Well, my hat's off to you. You're better than me."

Then, the three bumps signaling an announcement beeped, and Ms. Brown's voice reminded them of the teacher's meeting.

He stayed close to the three of them as they got up and walked to the library. When they reached their destination, Ryan came to Faith's side.

"Will you be celebrating the end of the first day?"

"Yes," she sighed, "by climbing into bed, I might not even eat; I'm bone tired."

"I hear you. I'm going to Maggie's for dinner; we like to talk the first day over. It's our tradition."

"That sounds nice."

"Have you got plans for the weekend?"

Before she could answer, one of the third-grade teachers, Ashley Sheridan, came to the door, and glaring at Ryan with blue eyes, she tried to shove her way in. She gave him a malicious smile before turning to Faith.

"Ms. Rogers? Faith, right?"

"Yes."

"I just wanted to say hello and warn you of our very own school, Lothario," she laughed brittlely, "I see I'm just in time."

"Oh," Faith was shocked and silent.

"Some men are just players, isn't that right, Ryan?"

"Nice to see you, Ashley," his eyes flashed a warning.

"Well, I've done my duty. Just be careful, Ms. Rogers."

"Um, thank you?"

"The meeting is getting ready to start," Ashley tried to hurry Faith away from Ryan.

"Yes, I'll be right there," Faith swallowed a nervous giggle. "I guess it's a good thing I'm not in the market for a relationship," she told Ryan.

She felt awkward saying it, but she knew how dangerous a relationship could be. She didn't want Ryan to get the wrong idea after their lunch date. She liked him, and that could be a problem. He seemed nice, but that was no guarantee. Charles had been her dream man at the beginning.

"Neither am I," he winked at her, then, without missing a beat, asked, "What are you doing this weekend?"

"My parents are coming to town."

"Sounds nice. Have a good meeting; I'll see you tomorrow."

"Tomorrow."

She struggled to keep her eyes off his retreating form; he was definitely attractive, and she needed to keep up her guard.

His teeth ground in their sockets as he watched Johnson Elementary School from his vantage point across the street. His listening devices were planted outside the building, by the doors where Faith stood with her class after school. He heard Faith talking to her teaching assistant. They were discussing the policeman. Ryan Madsen. Faith was telling her about a lunch date with him. That rankled.

As he scanned the school, he saw the blonde third-grade teacher again. Her name was Ashley Sheridan. He had done his homework. He knew the names of all the school personnel. He had been keeping tabs since Faith had come to work there. He was a great detective.

Ashley walked to Faith and started bad-mouthing the cop. That was music to his ears. Faith had listened and then quickly gone inside. He overheard the woman telling the teacher's assistant that Faith was throwing herself at the officer. That made his stomach lurch.

Then he had an idea. He needed an ally. One who could be in school when he couldn't. Someone who might even be able to get him into the building. This woman clearly hated the policeman. Another plus. He would find Ashley Sheridan and bind her to him.

He could form a relationship with her. Not that she could replace Faith. No one could. But she could be useful. He knew just what to do.

He followed her home, and when she went out for a jog, he went too. She was easy to keep up with; he was in great shape. He caught up to her. He knew he was handsome. Faith had fallen for him at first sight- just like he had her.

He approached her when she stopped her run.

"Hello, I couldn't help but notice you as you ran by me. I'm Charlie."

"Do I know you?"

"No, but I want to change that. I hope you don't think I'm some creep. But do you believe in love at first sight?"

"What?" she laughed.

"I've never seen a more stunning woman in my life."

"Are you for real?"

"Please, come out with me. We can meet in any public place you like. Coffee shop around the corner?"

"I don't know."

"I can't let you go without knowing your name."

"It's Ashley," she laughed.

"So, coffee?"

"I guess there's no harm in that."

It had been simple after that. It was so easy to win her that he was bored. But now he had an ally. She was his in. From here on out, it would be easier to keep tabs on Faith and the cop.

All that mattered was getting Faith back. He would do anything to have Faith, even if it hurt her. Sometimes, pain was necessary to achieve happiness. Soon, his plans would come together. Soon, he would have Faith back in his arms and never let her go.

Chapter 4

It was Friday, and Ryan had things to do. He shook his head in irritation. Instead, he was looking down the hall toward the Pre-K room. What was he thinking?

He'd told Maggie he was too smart to get involved with a teacher and asked her out the next thing he knew. He said to himself that he had just been trying to be friendly. But he knew that was a lie. He must be weak. Sure, she was pretty, but there was something else about her. He liked her. He told himself that the lunch they'd had was it. One and done. And then he'd asked her out twice. Fortunately, she'd turned him down. He reasoned with himself that it was better that way.

Why couldn't he keep away from her? He'd have lunch in the break room every day because he knew she'd be there. He enjoyed watching her try to eat her sandwich while she worked. Yes, she was every bit as funny as she claimed. He was beginning to look forward to their short talks while she multi-tasked. His lunch break quickly became one of his favorite times of the day.

He forced himself to remember how his mother had looked as she lay on the hospital bed. He faced the pain in his heart that still ached. He knew that he shouldn't let himself be vulnerable again. That would only lead to pain.

Faith was headed his way. Mandee intercepted her partway down the hall.

Now, he watched and listened to Faith and Mandee, one of the fifth-grade teachers, as they talked. It was hard not to admire Faith's figure. He liked her dark hair flowing down to her shoulders and her bangs setting off her big brown eyes.

He didn't even care that he was eavesdropping. He wanted to hear whatever Faith had to say. When their conversation registered, he came up with a plan—a compromise. Ryan wasn't ready to stop trying to go out with her. Maybe they could date, just not seriously. It's just something to scratch the itch. The more he got to know her, the more he wanted to be with her. She'd said she didn't want a relationship, nor did he. Maybe this might work.

He hoped she would be okay with another date to see if she wanted to play around. He didn't think she was the type to take to bed, but that wasn't what he wanted. He just wanted someone to help him with his loneliness and boredom. He felt a smile. This could be what he needed.

He turned his attention back to the two women.

"I wanted to let you know about our Friday Outings," informed Mandee with curious, bright green eyes.

"Outings?"

"We all go out on Fridays after school. I wanted to invite you. Tonight, we're going Mexican at El Charros on 71st. We'll meet at five-ish."

"Sure, thanks. I'm so sorry. Can you remind me of your name? I'm terrible with names."

"Sure, sweetie, it's Mandee Davenport; please call me Mandee."

"Ok, Mandee, I'll think about it,"

"Oh, hey, Ryan! I'm inviting you… again. You are part of our Johnson family. See you, sweetie, hopefully!" she smiled warmly and all inclusively, then returned to her classroom.

"Faith, are you going to the Outing?" he winked conspiratorially.

"Yes, I think I will go tonight. Sounds like fun, and I don't have a show until next Friday night,"

"Are you planning on watching anything special?" Did she have a date with someone else?

"No, not watching a show- performing in one."

"You're a performer? What kind?" he sounded surprised.

"I'm an actress and an improv artist," she beamed with a cocky tip of her head.

"Improv?"

"You know, improvisational theater. Games and scenes with no script just made up out of thin air, whatever pops into your head, you say and do. I just got back into it. It's so much fun," her eyes lit up as she explained it.

"You make it sound that way. So, Friday Outing?"

"Will I see you there?" she sounded hopeful.

"Yes, Faith, I think you will," this was the perfect chance to get to know her outside of the school setting.

It would be a little bit like a date.

He usually spent his weekends with Maggie. She'd drag him to church, and then they'd have a big dinner afterward; sometimes, her sons, wives, and girlfriends would be there. He enjoyed spending time with her. She was the only family he had. Her son Doyle, a detective on the force, was an old friend, but it was Maggie he loved. She had been there for him on that horrible day. Once again, he saw his mom's sweet face as she lay still in the casket. It had been so sudden.

He was getting morbid. He needed someone like Faith to help him get his mind off things. He was feeling lonely and wanted the distraction. Spending time with her was just what he needed. He finally let himself imagine what it would be like to kiss her. He couldn't wait for five o'clock.

The spicy smell of the salsa and cheese sauce at the restaurant surrounded them as they were all eating, laughing, and talking. Faith was thinking of Ryan again, much more than was healthy. She needed to beware. She'd fallen for Charles early on, too.

The feeling of being watched nagged at her again. She clenched her fists. Her anxiety was making it hard to breathe. She could see Charles in her mind, his blonde hair slicked back on his head and his intense emerald eyes glowering down at her.

Ashley Sheridan, the blonde third-grade teacher, had a gloating smile and cast superior glances at Ryan.

"Well, friends, I have news! I met the neatest guy. We've already been on one date; he told me he fell in love with me the moment he saw me. Talk about sweeping a girl off her feet! We're going out again tomorrow night." She looked pointedly at Ryan, "He is gorgeous! He's tall, dark, and handsome. Exactly my dream, man."

"Awesome! That is great. So, what's his name?" Mandee asked in a friendly manner.

"His name is Charlie Meridian; he's new in town."

"Cool," Mandee said.

For some reason, she couldn't put her finger on it. That name chilled Faith to the bone, and she shivered.

"Faith, are you getting cold?" Ryan gave her a quick look of concern.

"No, just a flidget."

"Flidget?" there was an amused look in Ryan's blue eyes.

"It's my own word; when you get a big chill up and down your spine, you do a full body twitch. I never know why they happen; they just do. So, a friend and I made up the word in grade school, and I never stopped calling them that. I guess I'm a little crazy."

While she was talking, Ryan was focused entirely on her; he seemed to be hanging onto every ridiculous word.

"I guess so," Ashley frowned at her slightly, her eyebrows in an angry slant, and Faith didn't know why. Did Ashley think she was a weirdo because she had chills?

"Well, ladies and gents, not to change the subject, but you should have been in my class today. The kids were insane! You'll never believe what Daysha was saying…," and Mandee took the conversation in a friendlier direction, in true teacher fashion, talking about the kids in her class; it was obvious she cared about all of them, even the troublemakers.

Soon after, Faith began telling a story about one of her favorite students, Damiana. Now that she'd stopped crying every day, Faith could see how sweet the little girl was. She recalled how Damiana led the other little girls in a silly dance and singing to the latest pop song. The whole group was laughing; she felt empowered. Making other people laugh energized her and made her almost feel electric. She saw that Ryan was laughing along with everyone else. She felt pleased that she was making Ryan laugh. His eyes twinkled as he caught her eye. As she watched him laugh, she couldn't help but imagine those smiling lips on hers. That made her giggle louder to dispel the picture from her mind. If she didn't stop thinking about his lips, she might forget how dangerous relationships could be. She was sure that her life plan wouldn't include a man. Yet, Ryan seemed different.

Why was her face always so expressive? Everything she felt she showed there. It was a little embarrassing. She knew he must be able to tell she thought he was handsome. Right at that minute, she was thinking exactly how good-looking he was. He looked straight at her, gave her a knowing smile, then gave her a subtle salute with his glass. She momentarily wished that the ground would swallow her up. He caught her checking him out; she wouldn't be surprised if she had been drooling. Get ahold of yourself, Faith!

They all started for their cars in the heavy heat at the end of their get-together. "Faith, let me walk you to your car?" Ryan asked.

"Okay, it's a blue Subaru Impreza."

"I know; we had lunch together on your first day at Johnson. It was our first date. I hope you haven't forgotten. Tonight has been fun, too."

"Yes, it was fun. You did seem to be enjoying yourself."

"You can tell a great story."

"Thank you, it's got to be my acting experience," she bragged as they walked through the parking lot.

"You must be a great actress. I was extremely entertained."

"Well, thank you. Oh, here's my car," she stopped at the blue Subaru.

"I know, too bad," he caught her eyes with his.

Faith felt her cheeks heat, and she stuttered, "Oh, well, I guess we're here, at my car… I mean, this is my car… of course, you knew that, because …um uh- date and um… yeah, well, I guess I should… go," she was acting like an idiot, just because he was standing so close. She took an unsteady breath.

"I think we've established that we know that this is your car," he smirked, "Be safe; I'll see you on Monday," he stood there momentarily, not moving. He was focused on her mouth, and he smiled. It was confusing and made her slightly nervous, but in a good way.

She thought he might kiss her, but he had just waved and walked to his motorcycle. She felt a pang of disappointment and chastised herself. The last thing she needed was to be involved with him. Ashley had warned her that he was a player.

But she felt so safe with him. She'd pray about it; if he asked her again, she would consider going out with him as friends. It could be lots of fun. She was sure she could trust him… almost.

Chapter 5

Ryan felt his lips curve into a wide smile; he always enjoyed hearing Faith laugh. Her laugh was almost a cackle; it was loud and raucous, and he caught himself laughing whenever she laughed. He was sitting on the covered patio at one of the local Italian restaurants, trying not to watch Faith; he kept trying not to think about her. He looked at the hanging plants, all shades of red and purple. But it was pointless; he couldn't help it. She was captivating. Ryan was always fascinated by her; he had been since the moment he met her. She was a ball of energy, a perpetual motion machine. Everything about her was fun and exciting.

Faith seemed unusually excited. He wondered what could be happening tonight that would ramp her up with so much energy. He hoped she wasn't excited because of a date with someone else. The idea of her going out with another guy made him feel disappointed. He still hadn't had his chance to make a real play for her.

He had a plan in mind for tonight. He was going to try again to ask her out. Ryan was determined to make her see the benefits of playing around with him. He hoped she would say yes.

"Well, everyone, I've got a show tonight. You should know; I sent tons of email invites to it and talked about it till I'm sure you're sick of hearing about it. I promise it will be *so* much fun! Improv is amazing! We keep it clean so that you can bring your kids! It would be awesome to see you there," she laughed and said, "I'd love to have y'all come,"

That was what she seemed nervous about. He remembered she'd said something about it last week. She talked about her group at lunch. He took a breath of relief. There was no other guy. Of course, that didn't mean she would be interested in going out with him.

Maybe he could see what was hiding in her day-to-day persona if he watched her perform. To see another side of her would be fun. This could be just the chance he needed to ask her out. He would go and then ask her out after the show.

Angel released an exasperated sigh, "I wish I could, but I don't have a babysitter tonight; my husband has already texted me ten times; the kids are driving him nuts," and she shook her head.

"I can't; I've got a *date* tonight," said Ashley with a smug, purse-lipped look at Ryan. "I'm going out with Charlie tonight. He is so thoughtful and unlike some men," she glowered at Ryan, "he loves to hear all about my day; he even cares about my job. He loves the school gossip as much as I do. I've never gone out with such a good listener. It's so refreshing to spend time with a man like that."

When Ashley spoke, Ryan saw a flash of fear in Faith's eyes. Was she afraid of Ashley? Why would she be frightened of Ashley? Was Ashley being unpleasant to her? He wouldn't put it past the woman. He knew firsthand how vindictive she could be. It was gone just as quickly as there, and Faith smiled again.

"I would, but my girls wanted to have a movie night at home," Mandee said, "Maybe we can come next time; I'm sure my daughters would love it. Next time!" she ate the last bite of her breadstick.

"I hope so. I think you'll like it. I love improv, and I think everyone else should, too. Sorry to be so pushy; I get excited," she apologized unnecessarily.

He wanted to put her at ease. She seemed uneasy. He caught her eyes again, smiling.

"Faith, it sounds like fun."

"Well, if you go, Ryan, then I'll go; I've wanted to go, but I hate going places like that by myself," said Maggie, with a little shake of her heavy silver-grey head.

Faith's face beamed. The sparkle was back in her eyes. He was pleased to be the reason she was smiling again. He just hoped they could get together.

"Y'all are going to. Yay! I promise I won't disappoint! Remember, it's downtown. It's across from Joe Mama's Pizza. The show starts at seven-thirty, and you'll want to get there early to give suggestions; it all runs on audience suggestions. This will be great!" she impulsively hugged Maggie first and then Ryan, and with a little jump, she waved a quick goodbye and nearly ran out of the restaurant.

They watched Faith practically skip out of the door. He was still tingling from the shock of Faith's hug. Maggie looked at Ryan.

When Faith hugged him, the warm, tingly sensation went from head to toe. He physically tried to shake it off, with little success.

"I'm leaving in a few minutes, Maggie, if you want to go with me."

"I drove here alone this afternoon, so I don't need a ride."

"As soon as we get our checks paid, we can go. We can walk there from here if you're up for it."

"As long as you're not in a big hurry."

"We'll get there in plenty of time."

"You'll have to tell me all about it. I hope to go next time. She is so funny." Mandee said in her usual friendly manner.

"I've always hated going to some community group performances. They are always terrible, and then you have to act like they are the next big Broadway star. It's just so annoying." Ashely's unkind words were jarring in the friendly setting.

"I'm sure it will be fun. I'm looking forward to it." Ryan was quick to defend Faith.

"Suit yourself. If you have a chance with her, you'll have to think of something nice to say. But a silver-tongued devil like you should be able to flatter her into anything."

"Ashley," his tone was a warning.

"Someone should really warn the poor thing if you're going after her."

"Now, you two be civil. I don't care what your history is together. There is no need for rudeness." Maggie spoke sternly.

"I'm sorry, ladies. I'll behave." Ryan said.

"I'm going. I've got a date to get ready for. Girls…Ryan." Ashley flounced out of the restaurant.

"Ladies, I'll see you all on Monday. Coming, Maggie?" he said, holding the door for her.

After the two of them left the restaurant, Ryan let out a frustrated breath.

"What exactly is going on with you, Ryan?"

"Ashley irritates me to no end."

"I know that. I mean you and Faith."

"What are you talking about?"

"For starters, you didn't start coming out with the teachers until she did."

"I'm not doing anything unusual. Since when has it been weird to hang out with your co-workers?"

"Since you and the whole Ashley incident. I thought you had learned your lesson.   You have feelings for Faith. I can see it."

"Someone needed to stand up for her."

"I know, and I'm proud you did. I just think it proves my point."

"I like her, but I'm not in love with her."

"Faith would be a great woman to get serious with. She's a good Christian girl; she goes to our church."

"I haven't seen her there."

"She goes to the early service."

"Oh."

"Ryan, why won't you get serious with a woman?"

"Maggie, you know about Mom; it all happened so quickly."

"Honey, I know you're still hurting."

"You can lose everything instantly. I learned that when Mom died. If you love someone, you can get hurt. Mom was here, and then, in a moment, she was gone. Why would I want to open myself to that kind of heartache again? Playing around is just easier."

"Well, Faith's the kind of girl who wants more than just a good time from a man. She seems like she wouldn't be happy with anything less than forever. I like her a lot; you need to leave her alone."

"I've talked a little about it with Faith; we agree. She told me she's not interested in anything serious, either. If we get involved, I'll make it clear that I do not want anything serious."

"But Ryan, think. You're usually very perceptive of danger. There's something else going on with her. Haven't you noticed that she gets skittish, with a look in her eyes almost like she's about to bolt? Something isn't right. I think she's scared of something, maybe of someone. Just think, ok, Ryan?"

"I can handle it. I'm a cop. If she's scared, I can help her. It's part of my job description. I keep people safe. It's what I do. I don't scare easy."

"I like Faith and don't want either of you to get hurt."

"I would never hurt her. Maggie, you know I've never hurt a woman on purpose. Ashley didn't understand the arrangement. I'll make sure Faith does. So, calm down, Maggie."

"I want you to be careful. You could be the one to get hurt."

"I'm always careful. Didn't you see how happy she was when we said we'd come? You've seen enough of her to guess it will be funny." Ryan smiled at her, offered her his arm, and leaning on it heavily, she limped beside him.

Maggie was the surrogate mother he needed. He missed his mom since she'd been killed. The circumstances had been so tragic, her death so needless. He had been lost. Maggie had, in a sense, adopted him. She tried to fill the void his mom's death left in his heart. He listened to her advice most of the time. This time was different.

"Maggie, I just want to have some fun. I know I can have fun with Faith. I want that, and I think that Faith does, too."

"Honey, I understand. Just watch your step."

They walked for a couple of blocks in companionable silence. Ryan kept remembering how Faith hugged him; she smelled like vanilla.

"If you are going to be my date, then we need to get a move on. I don't move as fast as I used to."

"Come on, Maggie, or do you need me to carry you?" he teased, "Wait, we're here. She said it was close."

It was a little grey building with a red door, just a hole in the wall. A giant red neon platypus was hanging above the door, wearing a top hat and a monocle. The edges of the sign were lit with large round lights, the kind that would surround a show sign on Broadway. The little window was full of posters for stand-up comedians and improv groups.

"This is a little small, but look, there's her picture on the poster. Why on earth do they have her in that blonde wig? I like her hair the way it is." Ryan complained.

"Oh, I didn't think you even realized when a girl got a new hairdo, that was part of your problem with Ashley. She had gotten a new cut and *color*; it was a big change. If I recall, you didn't even notice." Maggie gave him a suspicious look.

"I'm a guy; what did she expect?"

"I'm trying to point out that you've gone from being a *guy* to noticing that a woman's hair is different and that you prefer it. Concern about her hair is a big warning sign to me. You're getting awfully mixed up in the minutiae of this girl's life for someone who doesn't want to get involved. Watch yourself. You must watch your mind to keep yourself free of entanglements. Love creeps up on you slowly; it starts with little things that get bigger as time goes on."

"I didn't realize that noticing a woman's hair meant you were in love with her. I promise, Maggie. I'll be watching my step."

"Of course, if you and Faith get involved and decide to get serious, I would love to see the two of you together. Just watch yourself. Don't lead her on and hurt her later."

"I have never intentionally led a woman on in my life, Maggie! It's not my fault if they don't keep to the plan."

"I know. I know; it's just that this girl is different. I think someone has hurt her in the past. Just be careful you don't," she was serious.

"Okay, Maggie, I'll be good," he squeezed her shoulders, then opened the door for her, "Come on, let's see what Faith can do," he said, got their tickets, and they went to find their seats. He could feel himself getting excited. This would be fun.

He watched the show and couldn't remember the last time he had this much fun. He had been laughing more than he had in a long time.

Then there was Faith herself; she was dazzling. Her hair was up, her shirt was red, and her eyes sparkled as she performed. It was not only how beautiful she was; she was funny. She had turned into several entirely different people at the drop of a hat. Ryan wondered if all those personas were inside her all the time, waiting for the chance to come out. He realized he wanted to find out. He was sorry when the show ended, and the group bowed their final bows, then she blew one big kiss with a wave to the audience. He started to whoop and holler with the rest of them, and he stood up and clapped like mad.

In a couple of minutes, she came back out. She was shining, and she beamed up at him and Maggie.

"Okay, be honest; what did you think?" her eyes were cautious and expectant.

"Honey, you were so funny," Maggie said.

"I was… impressed and intrigued; I knew you were funny. All I can say is …wow!"

"Really?" she was jumping up and down excitedly and clapping.

"Yeah," he assured her. Then it was time to put his plan to work, "Hey, girls, let's all get a bite to eat. I don't know about you two, but I am hungry. We're in the middle of downtown; where do you want to go?"

"Well, let me tell my troupe, and I'll go with you two! We can go to Joe Mama's Pizza. It's awesome, and if you check the back of your tickets, there's a discount."

"Maggie?" Ryan asked.

"My car is up the road, and I think I'll go home." She looked sharply at Ryan.

"Faith, I'll meet you at Joe Mama's, okay?"

"Sure thing, Ryan. Bye, Maggie," she hugged her, "Thanks for coming to my show! See you on Monday."

"See you, Honey; you did a great job."

Ryan tried staying on alert as he walked Maggie to her car. He needed a clear head to keep an eye out for danger. However, all he could think of was Faith glittering on the stage. He cleared his mind of her again and focused on his surroundings.

"Hey honey, snap out of it," Maggie said.

"Sorry, I am just in the zone. Always alert."

"No, that isn't it. You have Faith on your mind."

"Maybe, a little, it's just that she is so… I don't know. I want to see what happens at dinner. I'm a big boy, and she's a big girl. We'll be okay, Maggie."

"I want you to proceed with caution. I love you like my own son, Ryan, and I like Faith. I want you to be happy, so move ahead carefully."

"I'll take things slow, but I do want to take things somewhere."

Chapter 6

As Ryan walked into Joe Mama's, the sweet smell of the dough greeted him; then, he saw Faith in a red vinyl booth. She noticed him and waved wildly. He smiled. She always did everything big. He waved and ambled over to her at the booth. He sat down on the bench across from her.

"Let me say again- *wow*! You are so hilarious! I didn't know you had that in you."

"Thank you, Ryan. You have now seen my favorite thing to do in the world." Faith laughed. "Why do you always make faces at me when I laugh?"

"I do *not* make faces at anyone."

"Oh, you do make faces all the time. I see you with the kids; you're always making faces, poor kids; you get them laughing, and then some teacher will get on to them. You didn't think I was watching, did you?"

"So, you *have* been watching me, and here I thought you didn't notice me."

"Whatever, Ryan." Her words were flippant, but her cheeks were pink. "You were sweet enough to say I was funny, so I'll tell you I think you're funny too."

"I know, I know, ha, ha, funny looking."

"Seriously, Ryan, a DAD joke? My dad has been telling those for years."

"Whoa! Stop now. Are you telling me I remind you of your dad? If this is true, I might as well hop on the bike and ride home," he said without any idea of leaving.

"That is *not* what I meant at all. You are much, much… uh, never mind."

"Not fair, Faith. If you're going to start to say something, at least have the guts to finish it. I want to know *everything* you are thinking tonight."

"If you must know, I was going to say…," she took a big gulp of air, "that you are… handsome." Her face was red, and she wouldn't look him in the eye.

"Thank you. You are adorable, especially right now," he was smooth as silk.

She appeared speechless. Her dark eyes were wide, and her rosy mouth opened slightly as if surprised.

"Now, tell me more about yourself. I know some, and I want to know more."

"Well, what do you want to know? Ask me, and I'll answer; not everyone gets a deal like this," she wrapped her arms around herself.

"Okay, Faith. First question: where in Texas were you living?"

"Answer: Dallas"

"Question two: Why did you become a teacher- you have a real talent that seems wasted in a profession like teaching."

"First off, thank you. But, it is hard to 'make it' outside of New York or LA, and I didn't have the money to go there, and there aren't a lot of paid acting jobs in this state. Also, I wanted to do what I thought would honor God. It's hard to get acting work if you're choosy about what you will and won't audition for. Besides, one of my college directors told me I wasn't the right body type."

"I think you are gorgeous; I wouldn't change a thing. But you have not answered all of my question."

"Well, since I knew Hollywood or Broadway were not in my immediate future, I also started working on getting a teaching certification in college in addition to my degree. I was meant to teach Pre-K or Kindergarten. Watching their eyes light up when they finally figure something out is wonderful. They are so sweet. No matter what you look like, you get compliments and hugs all day. I feel it's what I'm called to do. Now that I have found an improv troupe that keeps it clean and a community theater where I can pick and choose the plays I want to audition for, I feel fulfilled. I'm happy with my little ones."

"You make it sound like it's not all bad. I don't know if I could deal with the runny noses and wet pants."

"My class this year is precious. You know Damiana?"

"Yes, didn't she cry for two weeks straight?"

"She got over it. She's precious."

"She has a sweet smile now that she's not always crying."

"Just today, she told me I was a princess in disguise as a teacher."

"I didn't know I was in the presence of royalty," he said in a mockingly solemn voice.

"You should be honored," Faith laughed.

"Next question, and I've got a feeling you don't want to answer it."

"What?" she squirmed,

"If you don't want to answer it, you don't have to, but why did you move to Tulsa?"

"I should have known this one was coming," she took a deep breath, "I hate talking about it, but you ought to know. Let's say that I had a psycho… fiancé. He got… violent. When I broke up with him, he didn't believe I meant it, and things got… scary. I figured out that it would be better for me to get out of town. So, I returned to my home state, not my hometown. He won't find me."

"I'm sorry you had to deal with all of that. I've seen that kind of thing before. That explains a lot," understanding dawned on him.

"Let's say that I learned from my experience. That's why I don't date- it can end so badly, you never know about people… until it's too late,"

He didn't like being lumped in with everyone. He was a good guy, a good cop. He'd never hurt a woman. He wanted Faith to feel safe, to be safe.

"You can trust me."

"The only One I trust in is the Lord. I can try trusting you, but that's a tall order." she shook herself as if trying to shake off an unpleasant thought, "But let's talk about something else."

Then the waiter brought the pie; it was steaming, full of melted cheese and pepperoni. The smell was spicy and mouthwatering to the hungry pair. They began eating greedily. They didn't talk as they ate their first pieces, but the conversation started again mid-way through the second slice.

"Now it's my turn," Faith stated after she swallowed.

"Shoot. My life is an open book."

"Now it's my turn to ask you, why do police work? And why at a school?"

"I love police work; I've always wanted to do it. I like to help people. When the chance came to work at Johnson, I wanted it. My mom taught at Johnson till I… lost her."

"I'm sorry. When did you lose her?"

"Three years ago. She was… killed in a hit-and-run. I found out later that it was intentional." he couldn't talk about it.

"Oh! Ryan! That's horrible!"

"I don't like to talk about it."

"Sorry, I brought it up."

"It's okay. You couldn't have known."

They sat in a moment of uncomfortable silence. She cleared her throat as if to clear the air of the sad topic,

"Let's change the subject," he suggested, "Have you got another question for me?"

"Um, okay… satisfy my curiosity- that little scar on your lip, not that I've been staring."

"I got it in a fight; I was ten. Mom told me to stand up to a bully. I had to get a couple of stitches, but it was worth it. I've been doing it ever since."

"That makes you a good police officer."

"Thank you," at that moment, he wanted to kiss her.

There was a moment of charged silence as he tried to concentrate on something besides her mouth. The intensity of it seemed to force a giggle from her.

"I told you about my big, bad past, so it's your turn."

"What do you want to know?"

"I've heard some talk and seen her in action. I'd like to hear what you have to say about it."

"What do I have to say about what?" he was a little nervous.

"Ashley"

"Oh! I should have figured you'd learned about all that mess by now. Especially since I am interested in you," he looked straight into her eyes.

"Me?"

"You know I am, don't you?"

"I mean… I umm… you, well umm… me?" Faith stammered.

"Yes, you," he was smiling at her with a twinkle in his eyes. He went on, "So, I need you to know what happened. We started pretty much the same way. And I thought she understood that I was not interested in anything serious or permanent," he told Faith. She looked at him eagerly, inviting him to confide.

He continued his story, "Ashley agreed, and we went on a few dates, and one thing led to another. Then she started getting clingy. She told me we should get serious, and I told her I didn't want to. She threw a fit, and we broke up. She began a vendetta against me that is still going strong. Despite what she implies, I've never dated more than one woman at a time. I didn't want to get serious… with her. If we start to go out together, and I hope we do, I want us to be clear that I don't do forever," for a moment, he wanted to be serious with Faith, but they both had too much baggage to ever get with each other.

"I agree; I am not in the market for a serious boyfriend. That is not in the cards for me. I know that. I've made too many mistakes. But…" Faith was bright red, like her shirt, "I am interested in spending time with you, too," first, she looked down at the checkered tablecloth and then into his eyes.

"Then let's pay our check and be on our way," his anticipation bloomed.

Faith shivered. She shook herself and frowned as she looked furtively around the restaurant. She shivered again.

What was making her so obviously nervous?

"What's wrong?"

"It's n-nothing. I just thought I heard someone say my name. Did you hear it?"

"No," he hadn't been paying attention to anything but Faith.

"I swear I heard my name. I felt someone watching me."

"I'll take a look."

He turned on his cop vision and looked around the restaurant. He didn't see anyone suspicious. Then he saw the ball cap. It was just sitting on a table. It seemed odd. He looked at it again. Its owner had probably forgotten it. It was just that he didn't see many Texas Longhorns caps around Tulsa. He'd keep his eyes open.

"We're okay. You will always be safe with me."

"Sorry, ever since my break-up, I get nervous sometimes. You n-never know."

"Don't be nervous about me; I keep my promises." He smiled reassuringly and was glad to see her smiling again.

"Well, let me pay, and we can go. My card is in the black hole at the bottom of my purse."

"No, you entertained me tonight, so pizza is on me."

Chapter 7

He had paid their bill, and they walked back to their rides. The night was exactly right; the melting heat of the day had gone with the sunset. It was warm with a slight breeze, not too hot, clear, and cloudless. Faith stumbled over a crack in the sidewalk, so he casually took her arm as they strolled together. He helped her carefully walk to her car, gently guiding her where the sidewalk was damaged. He had parked his bike next to her Subaru. Ryan reminded himself that they both only wanted something informal.

He was considering kissing her; her eyes softly glowed in the dim parking lot. Ryan realized he'd wanted to kiss her all night, honestly, since even earlier than that. But he didn't want to rush things, which had been part of his problem with Ashley.

She was leaning against the driver's side door and looking intently at him in the moon's light. He could almost read her thoughts across her expressive face. She wanted to kiss him too, but she wasn't sure.

Faith was staring at Ryan, and she locked eyes with him. He slowly leaned in closer and put one arm beside her on her car door. He concentrated on her lips; he could almost taste them.

"Seems like a shame to have to say goodnight so soon on a night like this, but I've got a certification class in the morning," he moved in slowly.

"I have practice in the morning; we always practice on Saturdays; it's the best time for all of us even though it means I don't sleep late; I enjoy improv more. So, we practice on Saturdays… always, it's a good day to practice and more fun than sleeping in… on Saturday we practice-"

"You're doing it again," Ryan cut her off with a laugh, his eyes looking deep into hers.

"Doing what?" he saw her blush in the streetlamp's light.

"That thing you do when you're nervous," he grinned a teasing, little half-smile.

"What thing?"

"The thing where you talk ninety to nothing, and you ramble, repeating yourself. It's adorable. It makes me want to kiss you so bad."

"Okay," she barely whispered.

Then their lips met.

Her lips were softer than he'd imagined; he felt her body tense. He sensed her hesitation and surrendered control to her. She kissed him back. He knew he needed to stop first. He didn't want to push her. He knew it couldn't last forever, so he pulled away.

"Well, that was… nice," her words came hesitantly again.

"Just nice?" Ryan was a little disappointed.

"More than nice. I'm speechless. I didn't know you wanted to kiss me… are you sure?"

"I have been hoping we could get together."

"Together?" her voice shook.

"Faith, that is up to you. We'll go at whatever speed you choose," he reassured her.

"Okay, Ryan, I think I can do that. Just don't expect too much. The ex I told you about was … um, pushy? I'm warning you. Getting close makes me nervous."

"I'll go as slow as you want me to."

"There are things I just won't do. So, if you want to stop all this now, just let me know. I don't trust easily."

"I would never push you into something you didn't want to do. Don't you trust me?" he didn't like hearing that she didn't trust him, but he wanted Faith, and he wasn't ready to give up on her yet.

"I do as much as I can any man, maybe more, but trust is a tall order. It must be earned. I'm sorry, I still don't know you very well."

He promised her, "Then, I'll take it as slow as you want to, and we can agree to be only as serious as we want to be. I want to get to know you better," he saw her visibly relax.

"Well, I do have to go, I'm sorry to say."

"I would like to kiss you again," said Ryan, "Is that okay?"

"Yes," her voice was quiet but sure.

Then Ryan captured her lips again. He wrapped her in his arms, felt her tense, and relaxed. He picked her up a little off the ground. To Ryan's delight, Faith kissed him back.

Suddenly, Faith stiffened and pulled back away from him. Why? Had he spooked her?"

"What is it? Are you okay?"

"Did you hear that?"

"What?"

"I thought I heard growling and glass smashing. Do you think there's a dog on the loose?"

Ryan was instantly alert; his hand went to the gun on his hip. He hadn't seen a sign of any stray dogs downtown when he heard an anguished yell behind them somewhere in the parking lot. It was probably some homeless person and their dog. He knew there was danger lurking somewhere nearby.

"Ryan? Is everything all right?" her voice shook slightly.

"I'm not sure; I don't want to leave you to search for trouble. I'll feel better when you're safely on your way. We should both probably go home, not that I haven't enjoyed myself."

"Me too. But we both have early mornings. I hate to say it, but it's past my bedtime."

"You're right, Faith. I have that long certification class, and I want to see you get home safe."

A nervousness entered her eyes, "I'll get home okay. No need to worry; I can call you when I get home."

"I'd feel better if I followed you home just to see you get there safely."

"No!" she was forceful, "I- I- I'll be okay; I do this drive all the time. I'm okay."

"Are you sure?"

"Yes." She was firm, "But before we go home, I was hoping we could… um, classify... this? I mean, what exactly are we doing?"

"We can say we're getting to know each other."

"Will there be a second date?" she seemed expectant.

"There will be another date. When is good for you? Friday? After the Outing? Or if you'd rather, make it next Saturday night?"

She hesitated, "Would you like to come with me to a small get-together with my church group? We're having our end-of-summer get-together."

He wasn't sure he wanted to go out with a church group. He didn't mind going to the service on Sunday morning. He did that to keep Maggie happy. Going out with a church group didn't sound fun, but he wanted to spend more time with Faith. He made up his mind.

"Sounds fun. When is it?"

"Saturday night, we're meeting at the church at six pm."

"Great. I'll see you on Monday. Now, let's head home. I'll say goodnight," he lifted her off the ground and spun her around in a bear hug. He wanted to leave her wanting more.

"Goodnight, Faith. Drive safe. Call me when you get home; let me know you're safe."

"Okay. Goodnight, Ryan."

He watched her as she waved, smiled, and blew him a kiss as she drove off. As she left, he thought about his mom. She had thought she could drive home safely but never made it. After the suspicious activity, he'd heard he was worried about Faith. He needed to know she got home okay. He wished he knew where she lived. It was hard to wait for her call. How would he find her if something happened?

He decided to wait for her call at home. Ryan got on his bike and headed for his house. He headed down the highway.

As he was driving, he sensed that he was being followed. He looked behind him. Had he seen that car before? The dark Honda Civic was still two car lengths behind him.

Ryan took the next exit. The Honda took the exit. He turned down the surface street. The Civic followed. He wound around the streets. The car followed, always staying two or three car lengths behind. He couldn't call the station; he was on his bike. He didn't want to go straight home, but Faith should call him soon. He hoped. Ryan pulled into the parking lot of a gas station. The car went on past the Quick Trip. He waited for a few minutes. Then Faith called.

"Faith, are you home safe?"

"Yes, thanks for caring."

"Stay safe; I'll see you Monday,"

"Monday, I'll be looking forward to it. Bye," she ended the call.

Faith was the only reason he could think of for being followed. Could her ex be hunting her? But she had said her ex couldn't find her, that she'd escaped him in Dallas. Would the man have followed her here? That seemed unlikely. There were other possibilities for being followed if that was what had happened. He wasn't entirely sure about it. He decided he would alert the station when he got home. It paid to be cautious.

He carefully pulled out of the lot and headed home. He took the most circuitous route to get there, constantly checking for the dark Honda.

When he got home, he pulled into the garage. He didn't want his bike visible from the street. He sat up that night, checking the windows.

Ryan decided that Faith needed to tell him more about her ex. If he was the one following him, which seemed unlikely, then Faith might be in danger. He couldn't let that happen. He was a cop. He should prioritize her safety, even if it meant an uncomfortable conversation.

If he were dating her, it would be easier to keep an eye on her. It would satisfy both needs. He could stay with her, enjoy being with her, and keep her safe.

But what if being with him put her in more danger? Should he give her up to protect her? But he wasn't sure that he was followed because of her. He was a cop. He'd arrested people. Some of those people or their families could hold a grudge against him. He would talk to Maggie's son Doyle, the detective, about it. Get some insight from him. Until then, he could take Faith on their next date. He would be careful and not get attached. Part of him told himself that was an exercise in futility. By morning, he drifted off into an uneasy sleep.

He clenched his teeth so hard that his jaw ached. He had been watching the two of them. He was seething. Ashley had told him they had been spending time together at school and that she knew they were an item or would be soon. Ashley hated them so much that she was always glad to talk about them, complain, and spew venom. He hated hearing his Faith spoken about that way, but she seemed to set herself up for it by throwing herself at the policeman. Why was she betraying him like that? He knew she was his soulmate- she knew it too. He could still hear her soft, low-pitched voice when she'd told him she loved him. He could still taste her kiss.

He had ended his date with Ashley early, right before he came downtown, and saw she was doing improv again. He hated that she was performing again. He had never liked that. He wanted her for himself- he didn't like sharing her with anyone, not even an audience.

He saw the poster in the window. When she had run from him, she'd dyed her hair blonde. She'd gone back to her natural dark brown. She must think that he had given up on her. He never would.

When her show was over, he had discreetly followed the pair to the pizza place and sat in a booth nearby to hear them but not be seen. He needn't have tried so hard to hide- they only had eyes for each other. It curdled his blood to see Faith fawning over the policeman. He didn't know what she saw in the man. He wasn't her type at all. Faith had told him that he was her ideal.

He'd had to make some changes to his appearance. He'd grown a well-trimmed beard and mustache. He'd dyed it and his hair. He'd also changed into brown contacts and wore glasses. It wouldn't suit his plans for her to recognize him yet.

Then he felt the bile rise in his throat, and a wave of nausea gripped him as he saw them by her car. Then he saw them kissing. He'd never been a jealous man, but he was getting physically sick watching Faith kissing someone else. The sight of Faith's precious lips on another man's lips made him vomit. He spat and wiped his mouth. How could she do this to him?

He remembered their first kiss. It had been on their first date. She had been so hesitant and nervous. Her lips had been so soft, the kiss so innocent. At that moment, he knew she loved him as much as he loved her. It took her several dates to become as passionate about kissing him as he was about kissing her. When he finally conquered her, and she was entirely his, he began showing her the true depths of his love. It seemed now that she had made herself cheap and ripe for the taking, and Ryan was taking advantage. They kissed once more, and he retched again. What was Faith doing?

His heart was pounding, and he was seeing red. Didn't Faith know how much he loved her? She must have forgotten how devoted he had been. It was like she didn't care that he loved her.

He reminded himself to bide his time. She would be his again. She needed time to get over their last silly disagreement. It was why she ran from him. He'd been trying to make it up to her ever since.

He could give her all the time she needed to get over this stupid policeman and return to him. He would wait until the time was right to start slowly reminding her how much he loved her. It was only a matter of time, and he was patient.

In anguish, he had followed the policeman; it would help to know where the man lived. He wanted to keep tabs on the police officer. But he had lost him at a QT. He would find them both. Faith would be his, and no one would stand in the way of their happiness.

Chapter 8

"Evon, you'll never believe what happened this weekend!" Faith quietly told her teacher's aide as they sat by her cluttered desk at rest time. Evon was a big, black woman with smooth, caramel skin that radiated joy when she smiled or laughed.

"Well, I assume you and Ryan finally got together."

"How did you know? We're not dating; we're just getting to know each other, but we're going out again this weekend."

"Have I not told you for weeks now that he had a thing for you? The man can't keep his eyes off you. And you have been talking about him since we met. I've seen you; you turn red whenever he smiles at you. You better tell me all about it; I'm dying to know everything."

"Well, he came to my show on Friday, and then we went out for pizza and talked. He even explained the whole Ashley thing. But then he walked me to my car, and we kissed. Oh, my goodness- it was so amazing. I'm just worried; I don't want to make a mistake. I don't know if God wants Ryan, or any man, in my life that way. I need to pray about it. I don't want to get deeply attached."

"He is trustworthy. I've been at Johnson for a few years. I know Ryan. He can be trusted, despite what Ashley says. Besides, with a smile like his, I could figure he was a good kisser; he's got great-looking lips."

"Evon!" she grinned, "After we kissed, we talked about it, and we've got another date on Saturday."

"So, how serious do you think you'll get?"

"We talked about it. We're taking things slow; it might not go anywhere. Right now, we're just having fun."

"Do not get too attached. I know you. You might not be happy with something with no future."

"Evon, I told you a little about Charles. Dating opens you up to possessiveness. Possessiveness leads to violence. I'm not doing that again. I know that not all men are like Charles. I know Ryan is different, but I'm scared. I don't know where this will go. But, never again will I give a man any power over me."

"Faith, do not let an ex dictate how you live your life."

"I know you're right, but you didn't know Charles; he was a monster. I still have nightmares when I close my eyes. I was wrapped up in Charles' web for so long that I just wanted a chance to have fun again. Ryan doesn't want to get serious, so no one will get hurt. Don't you think I deserve something with no strings attached?"

"You do, but are you sure you want to be free of all entanglements? Especially with Ryan?"

"I hear what you're saying, Evon; I do, and I don't doubt the truth of your words, but I just want to have a good time with Ryan- with no consequences. That's why I'm taking it one date at a time."

"Faith, there is no such thing as *any* relationship without some kind of consequences."

"I guess I know that, but Evon, when I kissed Ryan, I felt like I was Wonder Woman and a fairy princess all in one. I've never felt like that before."

"I want you to think about your goal for this relationship and move accordingly. Pray and ask God for guidance. I don't want you to miss out, but I don't want you to get hurt."

"I hear you, and I know you're right. But can't Ryan and I just be?" Faith's voice wavered with frustration.

"Trust God. He will show you what to do if you trust Him. Who's to say God didn't put you here with Ryan on purpose? Faith, just promise me you'll be careful."

"I'm always careful; I just want to be happy."

"Pray about it; God wants the best for you."

"I will. I know. I'm just afraid to give my heart away."

Then Damiana raised her hand, "Miss Rogers, I need to go to the potty!"

Faith had to put the gossip on hold.

After their Friday Outing, Ryan walked Faith to her car, taking her hand while they walked along. The intimate gesture warmed her heart.

"I've been looking forward to our date tomorrow all week."

"Me too."

"Is it a dress-up kind of party or more casual?"

"It's casual. We're just going to have dinner and some games. I love card and board games. I hope you do, too."

"Sounds fun. Maggie and I play cards once a week. We get together at least one night a week, and of course, we go to church together and have Sunday lunch. She tries to keep me in line." He laughed.

"I hate to cut things short, but I've got some things I have to do for school, and I want to finish them tonight, so I'll be free for our date tomorrow night."

"I told you when we started this, we'll take it slow," Ryan said, looking disappointed. "Anyway, we're at your car, so I'll say goodbye for now." He took her hand up to his lips and kissed it.

"Wait!"

"What?"

"When do you want to meet me tomorrow night?"

"I'll pick you up at five thirty if the party is at six."

"Pick me up?"

"Yes, I figured we should go together, and I'll pick you up. Just give me your address."

"At my place?" she felt a tiny spike of panic.

"Is that okay?"

"Sure, sure, sure," Faith was hesitant about being picked up at her place. What if Charles found her?

"That doesn't sound okay."

"No… it is. I just usually don't let anybody know where I live. That psycho ex-fiancé I told you about, he followed me around after I broke up with him. I had to move a lot. He always found me and tore things up," she felt her cheeks flame with embarrassment, and she couldn't meet his eyes; Ryan would know how weak she had been. "Ever since it makes me nervous for other people to know where I live… you never know. He could have followed me here." Ryan was sure to drop her now. She braced herself for it.

"Faith, I don't want to make you uncomfortable. So why don't we meet up at the church?"

"That's okay; I…trust you."

"I'm glad of that, but if it makes you feel better, we can meet at the church."

"Thank you for being so understanding, Ryan. I know I've got a lot of baggage. If you want to, you can get out now. I won't suffer any permanent damage."

"A little baggage doesn't scare me; I've got some of my own. Now, back to the topic, which church?"

"Fellowship Bible Church."

"That's crazy."

"Why? I promise our church preaches the Bible."

"I know; that's where I go with Maggie. I should have remembered. I think Maggie told me that's where you attend, too. I was a little preoccupied at the time."

"Why haven't I seen you? Which service do you attend?"

"I go to the late service; I tend to sleep in."

"That explains it. I go to the early service."

"Well then, I know where to meet you. See you at six?"

"It's a date. Thank you for understanding. I'm trying to trust; it's just hard. Don't give up on me, please."

"I won't," his voice rang true.

Chapter 9

Ryan shook his short brown hair as he removed his helmet, leaving it a little messy. He got off his motorcycle and looked around the parking lot for Faith's Subaru. After hanging his helmet from the handlebars, he sauntered up the parking lot and to the doorway. Ryan had arrived early. He was dressed in faded jeans and a red polo shirt.   He hoped he looked presentable. He wanted to impress Faith and her friends.

He decided to wait for her at the party. Ryan didn't want to be pushy. He was surprised to see his friend Doyle standing at the door. Doyle was tall and blonde like his father had been, but he had Maggie's hazel eyes.

"Ryan?" Doyle asked with surprise, "It's great to see you! Mom didn't tell me you were coming tonight."

"I'm here to meet Faith Rogers."

"Faith?"

"Yes, she teaches at Johnson with Maggie."

"I knew she was a teacher; I just didn't know where she taught. She's great; we're so glad she chose our class."

Ryan felt a pang of annoyance. Was Doyle interested in Faith, too? Doyle had a girlfriend.

Doyle chuckled, "She's friends with Ellie. The two of them planned this party. I didn't expect her to bring a guy; glad it's you, brother. Why didn't you tell me you had a new girlfriend?"

Ryan relaxed and felt foolish. Ellie was Doyle's girlfriend. He was glad Doyle approved. Ryan looked up to Doyle; he was a couple of years older, and they had always been close.

"We're not really dating. We're just hanging out."

"It seems like more than that to get you to come to a Sunday School get-together. You haven't been to one of these parties in a long time. If I'd thought you'd come, I'd have invited you to one of these get-togethers. You'll have fun, especially if you're meeting up with Faith. She's so funny. She keeps us in stitches."

Just then, Faith walked in. She was stunning. She wore a modest purple sundress that set off her dark eyes and the highlights in her dark hair. She looked at him with a dimpled smile, and he caught his breath.

"You're early, and I'm running late. The sausage balls took longer than I anticipated. I wanted to be here when you arrived. I was afraid you wouldn't know anyone else here. But I see you've met Doyle."

"Doyle is a good friend of mine. He's Maggie's youngest son. I've known him since I was a kid. He and Ellie and I go way back."

"Well, I'm glad you'll know someone else here," she nodded at Doyle and said, "I've got some cookies and some sausage balls in my car."

"Let me help you with that." Ryan grinned, "I didn't know you baked."

"I don't often, but I'm on the committee. I can't believe I'm late. At least Ellie and Doyle were here to set everything up."

"You're not late; I'm just early."

They walked to her car, and he carried the basket full of treats back to the activities building. He was feeling excited. If things worked out tonight, they might start seeing each other regularly.

Ryan couldn't help but enjoy her company as the night went on. Faith was so much fun. Her quick wit made the games more enjoyable. Her friendly banter instilled camaraderie in the group. She was like a diamond sparkling in the sun. He was proud to be with her. The more they talked, the more he realized they had in common. The only thing that made him pause was how she spoke about spiritual things with this group. He wasn't used to talking so freely about Jesus. He'd always thought that those conversations were strictly for preachers. He usually blew Maggie off if she tried to get serious about God. He wasn't used to having to think about God except when the preacher caught his attention in the sermon. She talked about Jesus like a friend. He remembered when he'd felt that way back before his mom died. He wondered if it was too late for him. Would she still be interested in him if she knew just how far from God he had strayed? Was that a deal breaker?

He decided to ask her out again. They could talk more about this stuff. He also just wanted to spend time in her company. He couldn't believe he was spending so much time with her. He tried to remind himself not to get too serious, but he couldn't listen to his own warnings.

As the party broke up, Ryan decided to go ahead and take the risk.

"So, Faith, are you ready to end the fun?"

"What do you mean?" her eyes narrowed suspiciously.

"I just wondered if you'd like to go to that little diner down the street and get a burger with me? I've been having so much fun, and I had some things I wanted to talk to you about."

"Well," she hesitated, considering the offer, "I guess it would be okay. Ever since I got away from Charles, I've been careful. I know my mistakes with him, and I don't want to repeat them."

"I don't want you to be uncomfortable...."

"No, you don't make me uncomfortable; I trust you; I just don't trust myself with you. I made promises to myself and God before I got with Charles, and I broke them. I'm not going to break them again."

"No pressure. I just want to talk."

"I can do talking," she looked at him with a slow smile, "The diner sounds great."

When they pulled up to the diner, it was closed. Ryan hopped off his bike and went to her window. The look of disappointment on Ryan's face was like a puppy that had been left behind. She got out of her car so that she could talk to him.

"I guess I'll have to take a rain check."

"I hate to disappoint you."

"This calls for another date. I want to get your perspective on some things."

"Another date sounds fun," she was excited at the thought of another date with Ryan.

"The State Fair is coming to town next weekend, and I thought we could go together."

"Parking will be difficult."

"Not on my bike," his eyes lit up, "we could meet at the church, and I could take us on my bike to the fair."

"You could pick me up at my apartment," it was a risk but one she would be glad to take; she was starting to trust Ryan.

"Are you sure that wouldn't make you feel uncomfortable? I don't want that."

"Ryan, I trust you."

His face lit up like a Christmas tree when her words were out.

"Thank you. I'm glad you feel that way," he wrapped his arms around her, picked her up, and spun her around. She thought he might kiss her. Instead, he held her firmly in his arms and looked deeply into her eyes, "We can take it slow," it was as if he read her mind.

Suddenly, they heard a deep, anguished cry, glass breaking, and the alarm went off. Ryan was instantly in cop mode.

"Get in your car and stay there till I know it's safe. I'm calling the station."

Faith hopped back in her car without argument and locked the doors. She waited nervously as she saw Ryan walk around the empty parking lot, checking behind the diner. She was feeling afraid for him. She said a quick prayer for his safety.

As soon as Faith was locked in her car, he called the station, told them his location, and found they were already on their way in response to the alarm. He pulled his gun out of the concealed holster as he scanned the perimeter. The parking lot was empty. He circled the diner, trying to figure out what exactly he was looking for. Then he saw it. The back window was shattered. There in the broken glass lay a fractured cinder block. From what he could see, the glass had been broken from the outside. Who had been back here? Why? He wondered about being followed the previous weekend. Could someone have followed them here? Why? An ugly thought occurred to him: could it be someone looking for Faith? Was her ex here? He ran back to her. She was still sitting safely in her car. His heart started to slow down, and he was amazed to realize how fast it had beat. Ryan breathed a sigh of relief.

"Faith?" he knocked on her window, and she rolled it down, "It's all right. The police are on their way. Someone broke the back window of the diner."

"Are they in there?" her eyes were round with fear.

"I didn't see anyone, but the other cops will handle it. You are my priority."

Just then, the other officers arrived and started investigating the scene. Ryan felt like an idiot as he told the others his theory; they listened but dismissed it. He and Faith said the little bit they knew. Then they were free to go. Ryan was worried; he didn't want Faith to go home alone.

"Faith, can I follow you home? I won't be easy in my mind until I see for myself that you are safe."

"Yes, that would be great. I'm a little nervous. This whole thing seems strange."

He followed her through town, around the surface streets, and into a shabby neighborhood. He was surprised when she pulled into the parking lot of a low-rent apartment complex. It looked a little seedy. He hoped she was safe here.

After they got to Faith's apartment, Ryan got off his bike and followed her to her door. He watched her unlock several locks, then she carefully opened the door and looked around. She went cautiously inside and quickly swept the living room, which flowed into her tiny kitchen. She quickly and quietly peeked into the bedroom and ensuite bathroom, and he followed her lead. He felt like he was clearing rooms at a potential crime scene and gripped his gun tighter.

"Sorry, ever since my ex, I get nervous when I enter my apartment. After I left him, he would find me wherever I was staying. Once, he was hiding in my motel room. He took me back to my old apartment; I didn't think I'd ever get away from him."

"I'm sorry you had to live through that. You're a survivor."

"I don't know. Charles left lots of scars. I still get scared."

He looked around swiftly- cop-like, taking in his surroundings. Her apartment was almost empty aside from the few pieces of mismatched furniture; the walls were bare. He thought it strange that none of her personality was reflected in the apartment. It looked like she wasn't planning on staying long. He wondered how long she'd lived there. He saw unfolded clean clothes in a basket on the brown leather couch and a few dishes piled in the sink.

"Sorry about the mess," Faith mumbled, her cheeks stained pink.

"You weren't expecting company," he grinned, trying to put her at ease.

"I could offer you some coffee or some sweet tea?"

"I should probably get moving."

"Oh," her eyes drooped with disappointment.

"I don't want to impose or give your neighbors the wrong idea."

"Oh," her eyes lit up, "That is so considerate of you."

He knew he needed to go home because he was tempted to kiss her again. He wasn't going to push her, so he hugged her and said, "I'll see you on Monday."

"I'm looking forward to it. Goodnight."

"Goodnight." Then he hurried to his bike before he could kiss her and scare her away. As he rode home, he let the wind blow through him, hoping it would blow away these feelings that were taking him over.

Chapter 10

As he reclined on his bed, he sighed and put down the book he was trying to read. Ryan was distracted; he started drumming his fingers against the mattress. He hadn't realized until now how bad her last relationship had been. The man must have been a little bit psycho. Could he be the one who followed him last week?

This guy had followed her before. Could he have followed her here? She seemed to be afraid he had. He needed to investigate this. Could this ex find her? Would he hurt her? That scared him in more ways than one. If something happened to her, it would hurt him not just because she was a colleague, not because he wanted to play around with her, but because he was starting to care deeply about her.

Next to the bed was his graduation picture on his nightstand. He was smiling next to his mom. He thought of her. He wished he could talk to her. He made himself think about the accident. No, not an accident. They found out that the driver had been a teenager, just fifteen. The first day was over, and she'd stayed late to prepare things for the next day. The kid had been angry with her because she had caught him in the playground with his girlfriend doing something they shouldn't have. She knew the kids, confronted them, and threatened to call the police. The kid followed her in his brother's car when she left the school. Ryan didn't know if she had seen the kid following her, and he hadn't been allowed to ask many questions that day. The kid had run the car into his mom's coupe. It was one of those little gas-getters. The kid had t-boned it, and they'd had to cut her out of the car. She'd not lasted long at the hospital. He'd barely been able to say goodbye. The kid had been in critical condition, but he'd lived. He got tried as an adult and sent to prison. That incident was part of the reason Johnson got a school police officer.

Mom would have helped him know what to do. She was so wise. He wanted to keep dating Faith and didn't want to give her up. Not yet. Faith needed him; he could see that. She needed his protection, but did she need *him* in her life? He didn't want to think that he needed her. But maybe he did. Ryan came to a decision. He would stay the course. He wasn't sure he could give her up.

Sunday morning, she was up later than usual. She got ready for church in a rush and saw she would be late for the early service. She was disappointed. Then she remembered that Ryan might be at the late service with Maggie. She would take her time and go after Sunday School instead of before it. Maybe she could sit with them. It would be nice to enjoy the service with him.

When she got to Sunday School, Doyle was eager to greet her.

"I didn't know you knew Ryan. I was glad to see him at the party yesterday. He used to be involved with his Sunday School class before his mom was killed. When she died, he just pulled into himself; he just stopped. He would come with my mom to the service, but he wasn't the same. He shut down. The only person he really spends time with is my mom. He dated some teacher for a while, but I could see he wasn't invested in her. Mom said Ryan broke up with her, but he went deeper into himself afterward. It was nice to see him; he was like his old self again last night. I haven't seen him laughing so much in years. You're good for him."

"I was just glad he came. He's a great guy," she could feel her cheeks flush with excitement; maybe things could work out with Ryan.

"Mom says he's coming out of himself at work too."

"That's good to hear."

After class, she went to the sanctuary and looked for a seat. As usual, the simple beauty of the room filled her with peace. The light through the stained-glass windows painted pictures on the white walls. The pew she usually sat in during the morning service was packed. Then she saw Maggie and Ryan.

"Faith!" Maggie called her over, "Sit with us, honey. There's plenty of room."

"Thanks," her heart sped up as she came to them.

"Why don't you sit by me?" Ryan drawled and motioned for her to sit next to him.

"Thank you, that would be great."

"I thought you went to the early service; seeing you is a happy surprise."

His words sent bubbles of giddiness in her veins. She was delighted she'd decided to come late.

As the service began, the music started, and she felt joyful. Standing beside Ryan and hearing his rich baritone filled her with a thrill of happiness. She could get used to this. Their voices entwined in praise to King Jesus. It was beautiful.

When the pastor began to preach, she listened to his words. His message was about fear. About letting go of fear and not letting fear run your life. It was hitting home. She was afraid; she lived in fear. Fear was her constant companion.

The text was Psalm 91. As the pastor, a middle-aged man with a receding hairline that he wore slicked back, read it, she felt the Spirit's presence revealing the truth to her soul. "He who dwells in the shelter of the Most High will rest in the shadow of the Almighty. I will say of the Lord, "He is my refuge and my fortress, my God, in whom I trust… "Because he loves me," says the Lord, "I will rescue him; I will protect him, for he acknowledges my name. He will call on me, and I will answer him; I will be with him in trouble; I will deliver him and honor him. With long life, will I satisfy him and show him my salvation."

She had lied to herself about Charles; she thought she could change him. She felt he wouldn't be that way if she loved him enough and gave him what he wanted. If she were just a better person, she could save him. Those thoughts were all lies he told her. He was a narcissist and a psychopath.

Why had she stayed with him so long? Why had she given herself to him? She had repented, but she was still paying for it. She was still filled with guilt. Sometimes, she wondered if she was still under His shadow, safe in His wings.

She reminded herself that she had been strong. She had left him. It was God who had given her that strength and God who had forgiven her. It was God who would keep her safe.

Yes, she was in trouble, but God loved her, and she acknowledged His name. She could call on him in her times of fear and danger. She remembered that God had put her here in this place. God would protect her.

She had renewed her vows and had decided not to pursue any new romantic relationships. She was sure that she had blown that chance. But now there was Ryan. She felt that maybe God was putting them together for a reason.

Faith believed that God had put her at Johnson. Ryan was there like an angel sent to guard her. God had placed her under Ryan's protection. Had God also put Ryan in her heart?

Faith said a quick prayer of thanksgiving to God for keeping her safe and putting her in Ryan's path. When she had prayed, she stole a glance at Ryan. There was a look of concentration on his face, and he was so absorbed that he didn't catch her searching looks at him.

Ryan was usually distracted during the sermon, looking at the beautiful stained-glass windows or sometimes secretly scrolling through his phone. His mind wandered, and all his negative thoughts would creep in. Today, he had to pretend at least to pay attention because Faith was sitting beside him. His thoughts were starting to stray. Then, the message caught his ear. "The peace of God that transcends all understanding will guard your hearts and your minds in Christ Jesus." Peace? He needed peace. His brain was constantly whirling, always seeing the worst-case scenarios. His mind was always full of worries and anxieties. He was so afraid of losing the ones he cared about. Ryan had no peace since his mother's death.

He was a Christian; he had to admit he had strayed from God. Could that be why he had no peace? Was his anger at God causing all his mental turmoil? He'd willfully turned from God when his mom died. He certainly hadn't guarded his mind; he'd fallen into sin. Could he come back from that? Could he have that peace?

He knew he'd definitely sinned with Ashley. He had given in to his passions and hadn't kept himself pure. He'd never even considered a long-term relationship with her. He had only been out for himself. Could he return to God and get the peace he desperately needed? He needed to think about this. He wished he could talk with his mom about it; maybe Maggie could help him understand.

Ryan glanced over at Faith, who was also listening attentively. She had tears in her eyes. He reached over and squeezed her hand. Then he caught her eye, and she smiled at him, her eyes shining. Was she looking for peace, too?

When the service was over, Maggie looked at him and winked. Then she turned to Faith and asked, "Honey, we always have Sunday dinner at my house, and I would love to have you join us."

"I couldn't impose."

"Nonsense. I always cook enough to feed an army; that's what Ryan tells me. Today, it was just going to be Ryan and me. My other sons have other plans."

Ryan felt a rush of love for Maggie; she included him as her son. She always made him feel like family.

"I don't know,"

"I insist," Maggie pushed.

"Please come, Faith." Ryan gave her his puppy dog eyes again.

There was a moment of hesitation, and then she smiled and acquiesced.

"Would you like to follow Maggie, or would you mind riding with me? I left the bike at home."

"I'd be glad to ride with you."

Ryan couldn't hide his excitement. Time with Faith and Maggie should be lots of fun. He would get to spend more time with Faith; that would be wonderful.

He focused his binoculars and let out a low growl. She was at church. He hated that she was going to church again. She started pulling away from him when she began attending church in Dallas. She'd been a Christian when they met, but he'd slowly worked to get her away from that nonsense. Why she needed that crutch, he didn't know. Probably because she was weak, that was why she needed him. He'd become whom she leaned on. She was away from her family. She didn't have many friends. But all she needed was him.

His mind went back to the first time he saw her. He knew that she was his. He had seen her at her school; he was doing some community service at his job. One of the companies he owned had adopted her school and helped, donating supplies and snacks and volunteering with youth programs. He was working with the volunteers, and she appeared. Her short dark brown hair bounced in a bob. Her dark eyes flashed as she laughed at something. Her sashay was bouncy as she walked toward him. He was struck. In a flash, he knew that he loved and wanted her; she would belong to him.

He was a wealthy man, and he had captivated her. He'd spoiled her. He had given into her every whim. It had delighted him to take care of her that way. He wanted to be her everything.

He was a chameleon. He knew he could be whatever she wanted till he could show her his true self. He'd slowly pulled her away from her church, friends, and family. Eventually, she was his alone. They had only had each other, only needed each other. He'd owned her body and soul.

Then she'd gone to church with a new woman from her school. She'd done it when he was out of town. Otherwise, he'd have put his foot down. He'd been out of town for a week on business. He'd left her behind because she'd displeased him. He'd taught her that actions had consequences. He knew he shouldn't have left her alone for so long. When he got back, she was different. She was less pliable; she'd disobeyed him and denied him. When he finally had to discipline her, she ran.

He'd followed her, letting her know how much he missed her, loved her, and needed her. He may have gone a little far; he had become desperate without her. He'd finally taken her back. No one believed her lies and exaggerations about him. Everything he'd done was out of his deep love for her.

Her new friend had helped her, and she'd escaped him and then disappeared. But he'd found her, soon she would be with him again.

But first, there was a little problem: this policeman. Watching her leave the church with him cut him deeply, and he could feel the stabbing pain in his soul. He would follow them. As much as it pained him to see her with someone else, he had to know what Faith was doing.

Chapter 11

Faith sat eating at Maggie's big antique dining room table. They ate a roast with mashed potatoes, peas, and carrots. Maggie was an excellent cook, and dinner was delicious. Faith felt safe there. The big two-story house was in a small, gated suburban community. Plus, Ryan's presence always made her feel safe. With the Psalm still in her mind, she glanced at Ryan, confident that God had put him in her path to protect her.

Faith was having a great time. The three of them were laughing, and Faith felt a sense of being home. She hadn't felt this way since she'd last been with her parents.

Faith remembered that she didn't have her car when the afternoon drew to a close. She had ridden with Ryan. She needed to head home and get ready for work tomorrow.

"Ryan, I hate to break up the party, but I have to get home and make sure my school stuff is ready for Monday."

"Of course, I gave you a ride," Ryan grinned.

"Maggie, thanks for having me over."

"Thanks for coming. I'll see you tomorrow at school," Maggie hugged her.

"Let's go, Faith. See you tomorrow, Maggie."

"Don't forget your leftovers!" Maggie handed them both Tupperware containers with servings from the yummy lunch.

"Thanks again; now I've got lunch for tomorrow," Faith was grateful.

Then Ryan walked Faith to his truck. For once, she didn't look over her shoulder expecting to see Charles. She was safe with Ryan.

Faith thought about it for a minute. Should she let herself be vulnerable with Ryan? Should she tell him more about Charles? If he knew more about the situation, he would be more prepared to handle it if Charles found her and tried to make trouble. It might be uncomfortable, but she trusted Ryan. He would take her seriously. Hopefully, it wouldn't make him like her any less. She wanted Ryan to keep liking her. She admitted that she wanted a relationship with him. Maybe God was giving her a second chance to find love.

"What did you think of the sermon?" she asked as Ryan drove down the street.

"It was interesting. It really got me thinking."

"About what? Surely you aren't afraid of anything. You're a cop."

"I'm also just a regular guy. I have lots of fears and insecurities," he said, nervous and excited to talk about his thoughts on the sermon.

"You?"

"After my Mom died, I just got mad."

"I understand. It must have been a huge blow to lose your mom."

"I never knew my Dad. He died when I was too young to remember him. All I've ever had was her. We were a team. She kept me on the straight and narrow."

"No one can keep you on the right road but yourself."

"I learned that the hard way."

"So did I."

"I decided that since God had taken Mom from me, I didn't need Him. I willfully turned my back on Him and on the biblical teachings I was raised on. I started living for myself. I realize that is why I got into so much trouble with Ashley. If I'd stayed true, I never would have started the affair. I stopped keeping myself for God."

"I know about that. I let my ex talk me into… well… I gave myself to him. I had strayed so far from God, and I let him lead me farther away from the Lord. I knew it was wrong. But I was so wrapped up with my ex, Charles, that I followed him and did everything he asked of me. I let him rule over me instead of God. I've been paying for it ever since." She hung her head and got quiet as she shared her mistake.

"That has happened to a lot of people. It's hard to stay pure."

"But God didn't leave me there. I just repented of all my sins and rededicated my life to Him. I said I was sorry, and He forgave me. He gave me the courage and strength to leave Charles. What the pastor said hit me hard. I am God's child and live in the Almighty's shadow. I'm where I'm supposed to be."

"I was actually listening today. I want the kind of peace that he was talking about."

"All you have to do is ask Him for it. He wants you to have it."

"You need peace too. You also live in the shadow of His wings. According to the Bible, He will keep you safe."

" It made me think of you," she couldn't believe she was saying it, "I haven't felt safe in a long time. But you're right. According to Psalm 91, I should trust God. I think he sent me to Johnson because you are there. You make me feel safe."

"That's good; it's my job," he turned and winked at her, "I'm glad; I want you to feel safe with me."

"I need to tell you more about my ex. I think you need to know more about the whole situation."

"Okay, you don't need to tell me anything you don't want to tell."

"You need to know about him," she took a deep breath, "Charles is the only man I ever seriously dated. I was entirely on my own for the first time in my life. I had my independence. But I got lonely. I didn't know many people in Dallas; I wasn't faithfully attending church. When Charles volunteered at my school, I was bowled over. He was so handsome; he was a blonde giant. His green eyes still haunt me. He approached me one day and asked me out. He told me that it was love at first sight. I was swept off my feet. He was wealthy and treated me like a princess. At first, he said all the right things and did all the right things. I started to give in to things I knew were wrong. I let him take *everything* from me. I didn't keep my promise to God and my parents.

Once I started dating him, he became abusive. Mentally and emotionally, and eventually physically. Small things at first. I wanted to keep him happy. I stopped going to church. I stopped talking to my parents. I eventually gave myself to him: mind, body, and soul, and then he took everything from me. He gave me every material thing I could want, but all I got was shame, fear, and pain. It was a nightmare. I was trapped, and I couldn't get away. Then, a new teacher at school asked me to go to church with her. I started going in secret and got right with God. God gave me the strength to get out. I left him, and he became violent.

I moved. He found me; everywhere I went, he found me. Finally, one day, he was waiting for me when I came to my room in the motel where I was staying. He hurt me. When I finally got away, I went to a women's shelter for a while, then moved back home with my parents. I was still afraid that he would find me and hurt them, too. So, I moved here. I chose this place randomly, and he doesn't know where I am. I hope," she explained. By the time she finished talking, they had arrived at the church parking lot. Her story had stirred up all her memories, and she was tearing up.

"Faith, don't cry," his voice was tender, and he gently pulled her into his arms. He held her for a moment, giving her a chance to get control of her runaway emotions.

"I've been living in fear ever since I left him. But not when I'm with you. God showed me today that I am safe "in the shelter of the Most High and the shadow of the Almighty." Just like you reminded me, I feel safe with you around."

"I hope so. That's what I want for you. I want you to feel safe, to be safe," he hesitated as if he wanted to say more, "I will always keep you safe." He vowed.

"Thank you, Ryan."

"Faith?"

"Yes," she blinked her long, wet lashes.

She looked up at him and saw he was smiling again. He cleared his throat and shook the solemn vibe out of the air.

"Are we still on for the fair this weekend?"

"You still want to go with me?"

"Of course. I'm looking forward to it."

"Then I can't wait!"

She pulled her hands from his and opened the truck door.

"I'll follow you home. I'll feel better if I see you safe at your door."

"Thank you."

She was more comfortable getting into her car and driving home from the church. Usually, she felt vulnerable driving home, afraid Charles was following her.

When she got to her apartment, Ryan got out of his truck and said, "I'll see you tomorrow at school."

He walked her to her door and made sure everything was secure. Then he gave her a bear hug. It felt like home in his arms.

"See you tomorrow," he whispered. Then he watched her enter and waited at the door till she was locked in tight.

As Ryan walked to his truck, something caught his peripheral vision. There was a furtive movement behind the big dumpsters. Then he heard a muffled curse. He decided to look. He quickly retrieved his heavy flashlight from his truck and went to investigate. Ryan cautiously approached the trash bins. He searched all around and behind the dumpsters but came up empty-handed. Maybe he had imagined things.

When Ryan got home that night, his mind went on overdrive, and he couldn't stop the anxious thoughts that troubled him. He was nervous about Faith. Now that he knew the whole story, he was worried about her. He could keep her safe only when he was with her. And he wanted to be with her all the time.

That was also making him anxious. He didn't want a serious relationship. Or at least that's what he was trying to tell himself. He knew that he needed to pray again.

He heard the words of Scripture that had been preached come back to him. Peace would guard his heart. He just needed to talk with God. He'd messed up with Ashley. He'd hurt Ashley. He'd sinned against God. Maybe just praying wasn't enough. He needed to do something about the mess he'd made.

"God, please show me how to fix the mess I made with Ashley. I know that I can do nothing on my own to please you. Give me the strength and grace to confess and ask Ashley for forgiveness. I want to make things right. I want a clean slate. Thank you, Father. Please guide me. Please, let me know what to do about Faith."

His heart lightened, and he felt at peace. Thoughts drifted to Faith. He'd asked for guidance. He would give his worries about her to his Heavenly Father. He needed to get Ashley's forgiveness before pursuing Faith. He needed to slow down with Faith until he knew for sure if he was serious about her. With that plan in place, he could lie down and sleep peacefully.

Chapter 12

On Monday, Ryan was pacing the length of the hallway, agitated. He knew he had to approach Ashley, but it would be unpleasant. Ashley hated him. With his new perspective, he realized that he had earned it. He could see why Ashley felt used. He owed her this apology. He knew he couldn't move forward with Faith until he made things right with Ashley. He waited for his chance. He looked at the teacher's entrance, waiting for her to enter. She was always at school ten minutes early, like clockwork.

. The teachers' entrance came in through the cafeteria. The teachers could fill their coffee and chat briefly before going to their classrooms. He saw the tall woman enter, and he hesitantly walked over to her. He noticed that Ashley looked different today. There was something off about her. He looked again; her hair was a deep brown, and it reminded him of Faith's style and color. Were her eyes brown? He remembered her eyes being blue. What was going on? No matter what, he needed to apologize to her.

"Hello, Ashley."

"Ryan," her eyes narrowed as she said his name, "Do you want something?"

"I just want to talk for a minute."

"Well, spit it out; I've got to prepare for a writing project this morning."

"I won't take much of your time. I need to apologize to you," the words came out rushed; he burned with embarrassment and felt vulnerable, but he had to do this.

"Apologize?"

"I'm sorry for how things happened while we dated; I'm sorry for how I ended things. Looking back, I realize that I mistreated you."

"What?"

"I'm sorry."

"I don't know what game you're playing, but I'm with Charlie now."

"I'm not playing games. I'm just sorry that I hurt you. I shouldn't have let things go so far for so long. I should have been more upfront with you. I'm sorry I ended things that way."

"You were cruel. I loved you."

"I'm sorry, I just didn't feel the same way. I shouldn't have strung you along. Can you forgive me?" admitting fault wasn't easy, but he knew he owed it to her.

"It's too late now. I don't want you anymore. Charlie loves me."

"I'm not trying to mess up your relationship. I wanted to apologize for being such a jerk. You deserve to be loved. I hope you can find happiness."

"Thank you, I guess."

"Also, I see you have a new look."

"You actually noticed?"

"I almost didn't recognize you. When did you get the new hairdo?"

"This weekend. Charlie saw an old picture of me with brown hair and liked it. He convinced me to go a shade darker."

"With this new look, you and Faith could be sisters."

That earned him a frown. He didn't understand women.

"I'll see you later," he tried to be friendly.

She rolled her eyes at him and went to her classroom.

He took a deep breath. He felt freer after apologizing.

Faith was excited about her lunch break. She knew it was because she would probably see Ryan. She wanted to tell him about the strange things that happened after he took her home.

She saw him as she entered the break room with her leftovers and the folder games she wanted to laminate. When their eyes met, he gave her a heartwarming smile.

"I see we had the same thought for lunch. He motioned to the leftovers he was eating, "Maggie's leftovers are great."

"I'm looking forward to eating them."

She hesitated; she didn't want Ryan to think she was irrational. But she knew he could protect her. He needed to know if it was Charles.

"Ryan, I heard something outside my window last night after you left."

"What?"

"I thought I heard someone call my name. At first, I thought it was you, but I looked out, and you had already gone."

"That is strange; I thought I heard something in the parking lot."

Faith felt a sudden chill and a catch in her breath as she put her food in the microwave.

"Why don't I meet you after school? I can follow you home."

"There's no need to do that."

"I'd feel better if I did."

"Well, thank you."

Then the microwave beeped, and it was time to eat.

Ryan came to her class after school, as promised. But he had an annoyed look on his face.

"Faith, I can't follow you home today as I planned. My sergeant called; he wanted to meet with me about some vandalism in the neighborhood. I've got to go in about ten minutes. Will you be okay?"

"Of course, I'll be fine," her words felt like a lie.

After he left, she decided to stay a little longer in her classroom; she had some paperwork to catch up with. She felt a little uncomfortable with Ryan gone. She didn't realize how much his presence in the school eased her fears.

She heard a sound coming from the hall. She thought she was the only one still here down this hallway. Dr. A was still in the building. She wasn't alone. But the sound was still menacing. She quickly got her things and started to leave her room; she would finish her paperwork tomorrow. When she began to shut the door, she saw a slip of paper fall.

With nervous hands, she gingerly picked it up.

It was a simple message asking her to call an unknown number for a talk. She breathed a sigh of relief. Several of her parents changed phone numbers frequently. In this neighborhood, there was a lot of poverty. People would change phones when bills got too high.

She dialed the number on the school phone and waited for an answer. It rang and rang. Then the voice mail message said in an unearthly mechanical voice.

"See you soon, my Love."

She dropped the receiver. She felt a scream rising in her throat. She grabbed her bags and ran from the room, down the hall, and to her car. Charles.

When she got home and locked herself inside, she started praying till she could breathe again. She needed to be rational. Charles didn't know where she was. It was just a message. People often left strange messages on their voicemails. Had it been Charles' voice? It hadn't been. She knew his voice; she would never forget it. This voice had been slightly distorted, almost auto tuned. She tried to convince herself it was an innocent coincidence. What should she do? Call Ryan.

She had dialed his number before she could talk herself out of it.

"Hello Faith," his eager drawl started settling her frazzled nerves, "What's up?"

"I'm sorry to bother you at your meeting."

"My meeting just got over. How can I help you."

Now that she had him on the phone, she felt silly. He would think she was overreacting.

"Um… I just wanted to… tell you something. I feel foolish now that I've had time to calm down."

"Did something happen?"

"After school, I got a note… to call an unfamiliar number."

"Did you call it?" his voice had become business-like.

"Yes… that's the problem. No one answered, it went to voicemail…."

"Okay."

"The message was, "See you soon, my Love.""

"Why did that upset you?"

"Because of Charles. He called me my Love. After I ran away, he would leave me crazy phone messages ranting that I would never escape him. Sometimes, they were cryptic, but they always ended the same way, "see you soon, My Love." He would let me know he knew where I was. Inevitably, he would show up later and try to get in."

"Did you talk to Mrs. Brown in the office?"

"No, I just ran."

"She would know where the message came from."

"I should have thought of that. I guess I overreacted."

"Did you recognize the voice?"

"No. It sounded auto tuned. But he always called me "my Love." That was what this message said."

"Did you keep the message?"

"I think I left it on my desk."

"Is the phone number still in your call log?"

"No, I called on the school phone…."

"I'll look into it tomorrow. I wish there were more to go on. I can't do much without the number."

"I just lost my head. I didn't think things through."

"I'll do what I can. Don't worry; I'll be at school. See you tomorrow, Faith."

When the call ended, she felt better. There had to be an innocent explanation. Besides, Ryan would be there."

The next day, Faith found out that Mrs. Brown had taken the message. Someone had called and left the number. There the trail ended. Ryan had checked on her throughout the day and walked her to her car.

That Saturday, Faith was driving home from her improv practice. She had to go through downtown; traffic was crawling. Stuck in the traffic, she began to look around. She saw the quirky stores and the coffee shops. She stopped next to a little outdoor café. There she saw Ashley Sheridan, deep in conversation with a dark-haired man. Before Faith returned to the traffic, the man looked in her direction. For a moment, he locked eyes with her.

She gasped. The man's face was frighteningly familiar. That face chilled her to the bone. It could have been Charles' face. The face was leaner but with the same sharp nose and high cheekbones. This man had a beard and mustache. Then she saw the man had dark eyes behind his glasses. Charles was a clean-shaven blonde with green eyes. It still scared her. She couldn't look away, then the man smiled at her and gave a finger salute. She hit the gas in a panic. A horn screamed at her, and she slammed on the brakes. She had nearly crashed into the car in front of her. She started driving home again, cautiously.

Once she got home, she heard her phone ringing in her purse.

"Hello? Ryan?"

"Yes, it's Ryan; I've called several times. Are we still on for today?"

"Of course, I just had a bit of a close call on the way home."

"Close call?" Ryan's voice was full of concern, "Are you okay?"

"I'm a little shaky, but I'll be okay."

"Are you sure?"

"Yes."

"Okay, I'm on my way. You still want to ride the bike?" He sounded hopeful.

"You couldn't stop me. I've always wanted to, he wouldn't… I mean, I just never got the chance," she was starting to settle down; Ryan had that effect on her.

"I'll be at your place soon, Faith."

When Ryan got to her place, Faith was feeling better. She had convinced herself that the man she had seen couldn't have been Charles, and she'd reread Psalm 91. Its comforting promises calmed her fears.

"Hello, Faith. Are you okay? You said you had a close call? Is everything all right? If something scared you, I want to know. I can't keep you safe if you hold things back."

She told him of her strange encounter. He listened and said he would try to find out what he could.

"Now that is out of the way, let's get ready to go to the fair. I brought an extra helmet. Are you up for the ride?"

"I've always wanted to ride on a motorcycle. It sounds like fun!"

He helped her strap on the helmet, then they hopped on his bike, and he took them to the fair.

Being on a bike, they found a parking spot quickly. Ryan bought the tickets, and they went onto the midway. The combination of food smells had her mouthwatering.

"So, what's your favorite thing at the fair?" Ryan asked.

"I always love cheese on a stick."

"Excellent choice. I like the turkey leg, too. But what do you like to do?"

"I like to ride the rides, but Charles never let… sorry."

"What?"

"I don't want to think about that part of my life."

"Then don't let that ruin the fun."

"Okay, so I meant no one would ever ride with me."

"I'm game. Let's go get some ride tickets."

"You got our admission, so ride tickets are on me."

"Faith, I know that you are a strong, independent woman. But this was my idea, and I want to share it with you because I like you."

"I like you too, Ryan. I just don't want to be beholden to anyone, not after Charles. I want to stand on my own two feet, I like having my own money, I like the feeling of control."

"I thought you trusted me?" his eyes were big and blue as he looked at her, "I would never take advantage of you. I don't have any expectations. I just want us to have a good time."

"I do trust you. If wasting money on me means that much to you, then spend away."

"If we have fun, then it won't be a waste. Thank you for trusting me."

Ryan got their tickets, and they rode every ride they could ride except the spinning rides. Faith refused to ride spinning rides. When Ryan finally talked her into riding one, she ran to the trash can as soon as it was over and promptly lost her dinner.

"This is so embarrassing," she said after she was done, "I told you I can't ride those things."

"Don't be embarrassed. You warned me. You rode it like a trooper."

"Let's not talk about it. You'll always think of me as the girl who puked at the fair."

He just laughed, "I'm a cop; I've seen grosser things happen."

"Not on a date."

"You'd be surprised."

"Do you ever play the games?"

"I know a few tricks. I'll have to show you."

They went up and down the midway; the music was blaring, and the people on the rides were screaming. It was a cacophony of fun. They played games. Ryan won most; he knew the tricks to several of them. He got her a few cheap prizes and a plush cat. He even won her a giant stuffed giraffe.

"Ryan?!"

"What, Faith?"

"What are we going to do with all of this? We're on your bike."

"I've got it covered. I always carry bungee cords in my day bag. We can just put those little things into the day bag, tie that big giraffe to the back of the bike, and fly down the highway."

They rode in a companionable silence, looking around at God's creation. She felt like the ride was blowing away her cares and fears. She said a silent thanks to God for giving her this day. If she and Ryan ended things, she would always have this day.

"I've been wanting to talk to you about something," Ryan said as he walked to her apartment.

"Sure," his words worried her. Was he going to break up with her?

"You seem to have a real relationship with God."

"I try to."

"I want that too. I used to have it, but I got mad after my mom was killed. I was hurting, and I decided just to do whatever I wanted to," he hung his head.
"Is there any coming back from that? I realized that I needed to get back to God. Maybe that will give me peace. I haven't had peace since my mom died."

"There is always a way back to God. He is waiting for you. He wants to welcome you home. Like the Prodigal Son, God is waiting and will meet you on the road as you return to Him."

"You think He still wants me? I made some big mistakes with Ashley. She hates me and with good cause. I realize that I hurt her. I want to get right with God. How did you do it?"

"I just repented and rededicated my life to Him."

"Do you think he can give me peace again?"

"Yes. Just pray, repent, and ask Him. I understand because he did it for me. You can always come back to Him."

He hung his head and lifted his blue eyes to hers, "I'm embarrassed to ask, but would you pray for me? I've just been so angry. I know I'll only have peace if I get right with Him. I'd like you to help me, please."

"I would be honored to pray for you. I've been praying for you, especially since our talk on Sunday."

"I've started to, and I'm trying to make amends to those people I've wronged."

"That's wonderful."

"I wanted you to know I'm trying to make peace with Ashley. It's not going very well. I'm afraid she's going to come after you now."

"Why me?"

"Because I intend to spend more time with you," his blue eyes probed hers, "If you're okay with it."

She felt overwhelmed, happy, and a bit flustered, "Okay."

"Good to hear," he took her hand and led her to where his bike was parked.

She felt a flood of affection for him as he set the helmet on her head and tightened the straps. She looked into his eyes. He tipped her head up to his and pecked her lips.

She felt her cheeks flame, and she felt her heart flip.

"Will I see you in church tomorrow?" he asked.

"I hoped to see you in my Sunday school class. Doyle and Ellie should be there."

"I'll be there. Not to burst your bubble, but I'm not just coming to see you."

"You're not?"

"I'm also coming to get right with God. I want to have a real relationship with Him again."

"I'm glad."

They got onto his bike and rode through the night.

Chapter 13

It was Fall Break. Ryan and Faith were still spending most of their time together. They ate their lunch together, went to Sunday School and church together, and stayed after school together.

Someone still seemed to be hounding her. Ryan was worried about her. He'd called a couple of phone numbers with the same result. There were cryptic messages in that auto-tuned voice. It was unsettling. He didn't know what to do about it. But so far, it hadn't escalated. He was keeping a close eye on Faith and the situation.

He was becoming more and more infatuated with her every day. He told himself that he wasn't getting serious about her, but he couldn't seem to get her out of his mind. He told himself he was mostly trying to keep her safe, but he knew he wanted to spend all the time he could with her.

Ryan was going out with Faith and her parents. So, he was stressing a bit about it.

They were outside the restaurant waiting on their table and keeping up the friendly conversation they had started on the drive there.

"So, Ryan, how long have you been working at Johnson?" Luther, Faith's dad, asked him.

"I've been there for the last three years," Ryan answered, "I started working there after my mom… died. She had been a teacher at Johnson, and I felt like that was something she would like."

"That's so sweet! Your mom would be proud of you," Carolyn, Faith's mom gushed.

"Thank you. I strive for that," Ryan put his arm casually around Faith's shoulder.

"Faith said that you make her feel safe. She really needs that in her life."

"*Dad*!"

"What? You did say it, and it's true after all Charles put you through."

"Faith, have you had any more of those strange coincidences?" her mother was concerned.

"I keep getting strange messages from the office. It's a different number every time, but nobody ever answers. There's always something cryptic on the voicemail, which always ends the same way, "My love." It unnerves me; I'm so thankful to the Lord that Ryan is at our school. He keeps checking them out but hasn't found anything to go on."

"What do you make of this, Ryan?" Luther asked, "You're a cop. What should she do?"

"*Dad*!"

"It's okay, Faith, it's my job," he squeezed her hand reassuringly, "I'm keeping track of it, and I'm sending the numbers to the station. The messages come from those burner phones. But real life isn't like TV, and we don't have all the technology and manpower they do. I'm taking it seriously. I'll do whatever it takes to keep her safe," he vowed.

"Ryan, have you seen Faith do improv?" Carolyn asked quickly, changing the subject.

"Yes, she's amazing!"

"I finally have a fan. One who isn't related to me."

"I had so much fun at her show. I'd love to see more. If she wouldn't mind, I'd go to her practice with her," he looked down at Faith and smiled his most engaging smile. Just being around her made him smile.

"Thanks, Ryan," she blushed, "I would hate to make you sit through that. Sometimes, we get very little improv done."

"So, the most important question is, who is your favorite football team?" Luther asked.

"Sooners all the way. I went to OU." Ryan informed them.

"I'm an alumnus too!" Carolyn bragged.

"What do you do?" Ryan queried.

"I'm the Director of the Head Start for all of Pushmataha County."

"So that's where Faith gets the bug to teach the little bitty ones. How about you, Luther?"

"I'm also a teacher but teach high school Math."

"A teaching family, I've noticed that teaching runs in families sometimes, like it's genetic. I've never had what it takes to teach. I admire those who have it in them."

"So, did you see the OU game last week? It was a nail-biter." Luther asked.

"I try not to miss a game unless I'm out with Faith."

"She's never really liked football as much as the rest of us."

"Well then, Ryan, we're going to have to watch a game some Saturday; I'll even try to pay attention," suggested Faith.

"I have to warn you, Faith ignores the games. She usually has her nose in a book or is on her phone." Carolyn cautioned.

"I get more interested if I'm at a game live. It's harder for me to get invested just watching it on TV. If you really wanted to watch the game, I would be glad to."

"Actually, I have a few tickets to the game in a couple of weeks. I didn't think you would be interested, Faith. Would you like to come with me?" Ryan asked, "I have four tickets. Would you also like to come too, Carolyn? Luther?"

"That sounds like fun. We'd love to take you up on it."
Luther agreed.

"Now Luther, I'm sure that Ryan is just being nice. I'm sure he's got other friends that would be more fun than us."

"No, I was unsure who to ask to come to the game; my best friend on the force, Doyle, and all of Maggie's family are OSU fans. I won the tickets in a raffle."

"Well, if you're sure. It sounds like fun. Are you okay with that, Faith?"

"If Ryan doesn't mind, then I'm game."

"Then it's a date. We can meet in Norman early in the morning. I don't like to miss anything." Ryan set it up.

"I'm glad you're an OU fan. Charles was a Texas fan. We should have known he was bad news."

"Dad, can we please not talk about him."
Carolyn gave Luther a warning glance.

"I have to say, Ryan, you are a great guy. I admire anyone who can get Faith to go to a football game. I think you're good for Faith." Luther said.

"Dad, please stop."

"Faith, if your dad says I'm a great guy, you should listen to him," Ryan smirked.

"Anyway, I've been to plenty of football games."

"Only when you had to go in the high school marching band."

"Oh, my goodness, Dad, can you please stop embarrassing me?"

"I was in the band for a short time. I played percussion. What did you play, Faith? Probably clarinet or flute."

"No, I played trumpet, but I wasn't any good. I couldn't march and play simultaneously. I've got no rhythm, and it was hard to concentrate on both at the same time," she blushed.

"It's good to see you haven't changed. You can barely walk and chew gum at the same time. Sorry, Faith, but you are a bit of a klutz. You fell yesterday. I don't know why you insist on walking backward down the hall in heels."

"Oh Faith! Are you okay?" Carolyn asked.

"Only my pride got hurt."

"Remember when you fell down that flight of stairs and sprained both ankles?" Luther reminded her.

"I can't forget it. I took out two people with me."

"You were on crutches for a week."

"The only positive was that Geoff would carry my backpack." Faith blushed, admitting it.

"Geoff? This is the first time I've heard of him. Should I be jealous?" Ryan kidded.

"I haven't thought of Geoff in years. He was so handsome."

Ryan felt irritated; he wanted to be the one she thought was handsome. He was being ridiculous. That was clearly in the past. He was sure she thought he was good-looking; he had caught her checking him out just a few minutes before. It made his chest swell to think about it.

"You cried when he took Stacey to the prom," Luther reminded her.

"You went with your best friend instead. If I recall, you both had a crush on Geoff."

"You are both the worst! I should have known letting you meet Ryan was a bad idea. Have I no secrets?"

"I hope I'm not a letdown after a guy like that." Ryan teased, and her blush assured him that she liked him.

"Ryan!" she chided.

"No, the more he talks, the more I like him."

"Luther, stop. You're embarrassing her."

"I mean it, though. Ryan, I like you. It's about time that Faith got a good guy. Just remember- don't break her heart, or I'll break you." Luther smiled.

"Mom, is there any way to stop him?"

"No, you know your father. Luther, please change the subject."

"All right, Ryan, have you heard the one about the two nuns who walked into a bar?"

"Nope."

"The third one ducked," Luther laughed at his own joke, and Ryan joined in.

"Dad, seriously, not jokes." Faith groaned.

"Luther, what did the priest say to the banana?" Ryan's eyes sparkled with mirth.

"What?"

"I find you appealing."

Both men started laughing.

"Mom, they've started the dad jokes. There's no stopping them now."

"You can't break up with Ryan; your dad has found his soul mate."

"Mom, you're as bad as Dad!"

Ryan thought in passing that staying together might be a good idea. He saw Faith's red face and wondered what she thought of it. Then he just started laughing. Her parents were fun.

After that, the evening went off without a hitch. Ryan felt that he had made a great impression on her parents.

The four of them went back to Faith's apartment. They spent the rest of the night laughing and playing card games. Ryan relished the feeling of acceptance. Carolyn and Luther seemed to want to include him in their circle. It made him think again of his mother. She would have loved Faith's parents. He thought that Maggie would also fit in well with this family unit. In fact, after church tomorrow, Maggie would invite them all to lunch. He was looking forward to it.

When it got late, Ryan thought he should go home and get some sleep so that he would be able to get up for church in the morning. Faith walked him to the door, and he held her tightly. He loved how she fit in them; it was like she was made to be there. He bent his head toward her and whispered.

"Goodnight, I'll see you tomorrow. Thank you for letting me spend this time with your family," he said aloud. "Thank you, Carolyn, and Luther. You've given me quite an enjoyable evening. Looking forward to talking to you all again tomorrow."

He hopped on his bike and praised God that Faith's parents liked him. He wondered if he should finally get serious with Faith.

Ryan had gone, and Fatih was sitting on her bed, thinking over the day. The evening had gone off without a hitch. Faith was glad Ryan had made such an excellent impression on her parents. They had distrusted and disliked Charles; they had been able to see him more clearly than Faith had. She wished she had listened to their warnings. There were no warnings about Ryan. They loved him already. No wonder they did. Ryan was amazing.

She thought again of how naïve she had been. She had believed every lie that Charles had told her. She had given in to his every whim and demand. She felt the shame of it all again; she felt the fear. Tears escaped her eyes. Carolyn was passing by, and she heard Faith trying to sniff the tears back. Her mother came into her room and sat down beside her. Faith could see the concern in her eyes as she hugged her tenderly.

"What's wrong? Did Dad or I do or say something to upset you? Did we mess things up for you and Ryan?"

"No, you were great. I'm so glad that you both approve of Ryan. Things are great with him…"

"Then why the tears?"

"It's just that sometimes my past mistakes just weigh on me so heavily. I was so stupid. I messed up so badly. I brought all my troubles upon myself. Why didn't I listen to you and Daddy? Why didn't I listen to the Holy Spirit's warnings? I suffered so much and deserved it." she laid her head on her mom's shoulder.

"Stop it right now." Carolyn reprimanded, taking Faith's face in her hands, "This nonsense is just Satan. He is the accuser. God has forgiven you."

"I just feel like all of the things that happened with Charles are because of my choices," Faith pulled away and hung her head.

"There were consequences to your actions, but God has forgiven you and wants you to forgive yourself. He has plans for you to prosper and not to harm you, as it says in Jeremiah 29:11."

"I don't deserve someone as great as Ryan. I keep thinking that soon he'll see how unworthy I am. He'll come to his senses and realize that, and then he will drop me."

"If he doesn't see what an amazing Christian woman you are, then he's not worthy of you."

"Mom, you're a bit biased." she rolled her eyes, "I shouldn't complain; we're just having fun together and not serious. That's what I agreed to when we started going out together."

"His agreeing to meet me and your dad seems pretty serious," Carolyn reached out and patted Faith's hand.

"I wouldn't read a lot into it. He's just naturally thoughtful. He was probably curious, too. Besides, he misses his mom."

"It's more than that. I was watching him tonight. That man cares a lot about you. He can't keep his eyes off you,"

"I know he likes me. I just know he doesn't want to get serious."

"Maybe you both started that way, but his face lights up when he talks to you." Carolyn smiled.

"Mom, you're crazy."

"He's such a great guy and a Christian."

"That's why I just hate for him to be mixed up in this Charles mess."

"Now you're worrying again. Ryan is more than capable of taking care of himself and you. Besides, for all you know, that psycho is still in Dallas."

"You know I still have nightmares. I still have panic attacks sometimes. I feel like I'll never be right again. I'm sure Ryan won't want to get serious with someone as broken as me."

"God fixes broken things. Give it to God. Remember you are in the shadow of His wings."

"I know. I just have a hard time realizing that."

"Give God your trust. He loves you and wants what's best for you."

"I just feel so unworthy."

"You are God's child, you are forgiven, Christ died for you. His sacrifice makes you worthy. Thank the Lord that He sees Jesus in us because no one is worthy, just forgiven," Carolyn wrapped Faith in a warm hug.

"You're right, Mom. Maybe Ryan isn't my future, or maybe he is but I'm putting our relationship in God's hands."

"That's good. I'll pray about it, too."

"Now, let's get to bed. We have church in the morning. I'm also excited to meet your friend Maggie."

"You'll love her."

"I love you the most, goodnight."

"Goodnight."

After Faith went to bed, she prayed, "God? I need peace of mind. I need to be in the shadow of Your wings. I need your guidance. Help me know what to do about Ryan. I will give it to you. Keep me safe. Keep Charles far away from me. In Your Holy name, I pray – Amen."

She could rest and finally got a good night's sleep without the troubled dreams of her past. She woke up refreshed and ready to start the day.

Chapter 14

The day of the game was clear and warm. It hadn't gotten cold in Oklahoma yet. It usually didn't till late October. They had met while it was still dark for the drive to Norman. He was surprised to see a temporary OU tattoo on her cheek. Her lips were bright red to match her OU gear. She was so adorable. He wanted to take her in his arms and kiss her.

He opened the passenger door of his red pick-up truck, and she climbed in. "I'm so glad we're going to the game together today. It will be so much fun."

"I haven't been to a football game in years!" she said.

"When was the last game you attended?" he asked as he got in the truck and turned the key in the ignition.

"I went to see one in Dallas. It was a Cowboys game. Pro football doesn't have the same excitement as college games do. I like the camaraderie you feel with the others in the audience."

"Audience?" he laughed, "at football games, it's just called a crowd."

"They didn't even have a great show at the intermission."

"Halftime!" he chuckled.

"I know," she winked at him, "I did play in the school marching band. Halftime was my time to shine."

"I would have liked to see that. You in a uniform with a silly plume in your hat."

"Hey, you said you were in the band too. Didn't you wear a uniform and a silly plume?"

"Our band had berets for the percussionists," he preened, "and I look good in uniform."

"Yes, you do," she mumbled.

"What did you say?"

"Never mind…"

"You think I look good in my uniform, don't you?" he grinned at her, "I'm glad you think so. I think you're gorgeous."

"Thank you," a smile perked up the corners of her lips.

After they had traveled for an hour, Faith yawned big.

"Feel free to lay the seat back and doze. We're up awfully early. Would you like some coffee?"

"I'd love some."

"Reach back into the extended cab. I brought a couple of thermoses. I'm always prepared."

"Do you want one right now?"

"Sounds good."

"Which do you want? The red or the black?"

"Look at them and see,"

"They're engraved!"

"The red one is mine; you had them put the comedy and tragedy masks under my name. How cool! The black one just reads Madsen."

"I don't need things to be fancy. I'm a simple man with simple tastes."

"That's too bad; I'm definitely a fancy woman."

"I like that about you. Sometimes, you seem to sparkle like a gemstone."

"Thank you. I like your steady, calm, and unpretentious energy. You always help me feel at peace."

"I'm glad."

Faith opened the red thermos drinking spout and took a small sip.

"This coffee is wonderful! You know how I take my coffee! Heavy on the vanilla creamer. And is this flavored coffee, too? You amaze me sometimes."

"I'm just observant; it comes with the job, and I like it when you smile."

"Sometimes I think you're too good to be true."

"Go ahead and lean back, take a nap."

"Thanks, I will," and then she closed her eyes and, in no time, was softly snoring.

As he drove, his thoughts drifted to the woman at his side. He couldn't believe he was attending the game with Faith and her parents. He realized that this wasn't keeping a relationship surface-level. He was getting tied up in her life. Strangely, he didn't mind. He hoped she was okay with the way things were going. He didn't want to stop seeing Faith. He realized that it would hurt a lot if they broke things off. He tried to reason with himself that it was nonsense. He wasn't in love with Faith, was he?

He woke her when they were thirty minutes from the school.

"Sorry, I slept so long. I felt so peaceful with you that I had no bad dreams."

"I'm glad. I always want you to feel safe."

"Thank you."

"Now, what kind of music do you like to listen to?" he glanced at her.

"Just about anything, except rap. I don't like a lot of country, but I love Johnny Cash. I like alternative and praise music, too."

"You might like my playlist. It's a bit eclectic."

Then he pushed some buttons on his phone, filling the cab with metal music.

"I love this band!"

"I didn't figure you for a metalhead."

"I told you I like a little bit of almost everything."

"You continue to astonish me. Every time I think I have you figured out, you throw me a curve ball. We're great together." after the words were out of his mouth, he couldn't believe he'd said them. She didn't want a serious relationship, and neither did he.

They both got quiet and listened to the music as he drove down the road.

When they arrived at the university, they called Faith's parents, and met up with them in the parking lot about two miles from the stadium. They began the long hike to the football field. Along the way, they met the tailgaters and fraternity and sorority parties up and down the road. The celebratory atmosphere was palatable. You could smell the burgers and brats. As they went along, they laughed and joked, watching the pandemonium around them.

Ryan was enjoying the fellowship with her parents. They were easygoing, and Ryan felt relaxed. As they walked along, he held Faith's hand, helping her when the ground was uneven. He felt comfortable showing his affection for Faith in front of them.

At the game, he found out that Luther got serious about football. He only talked about the game, his focus tightly on the field. Carolyn was a little chattier.

"So, Ryan, were you in any fraternities?"

"No, I went to the Campus Crusade for Christ. That's where I got saved."

"I went there at my college too. If I had kept up with my Christian friends from CCF in college, maybe I wouldn't have ended up with Charles. Sorry. I don't like to talk about him when I'm with you, Ryan."

"The past is in the past. We can leave it there. You're here now with me, so let's just have fun."

"What else did you do in college?"

"I mostly studied. I was set on being a police officer, so I kept my nose clean." he answered, then asked, "What about you,

Faith? Did you do any improv in college?" he quickly changed the subject.

"I mostly did plays; we had a small improv troupe. I didn't get fully involved with improv until after college. I found a couple of troupes in Dallas while doing some community theater. I remembered what fun it was, so I joined one. After that, I had such a blast and was learning so much that I decided to focus more on improv. Especially because Charles got so angry when I performed in a play; he said that it took too much time away from him."

"I'm surprised a strong woman like you put up with that," Ryan said.

"I haven't always been strong. I'm not sure that I am now. I don't want to talk about Charles. I wish he would stop coming up in conversations. Let's watch the game. Are we close to a touchdown?"

"No, Faith, we're on defense. The other team has the ball," he laughed at her, "Didn't you learn about football when you were at the games in high school?"

"I didn't really pay attention; I was always too busy socializing with my friends."

After the Sooners got the ball and scored a touchdown and extra point, the jumbotron started their kiss cam, and Ryan took advantage of the opportunity. He grabbed Faith and kissed her playfully on the cheek. Then, when their picture was flashed on the screen, he quickly kissed her lips.

"Ryan!"

"Don't you think the crowd deserved a show?"

"Ryan! In front of my parents and everyone?"

"Look over at your mom; she's smiling. I don't think they mind," he said, and he kissed her cheek again.

After he kissed her, he suddenly felt a malevolent glare. Someone was watching him. He quickly looked around. He heard a low feral growl. Then he saw the man for a fleeting moment. Only for an instant, he saw in his periphery a sudden movement. He didn't get a good look, just the impression of dark hair. It was hard to see anything else in a sea of red and white.

His cop reflexes kicked in, and he pulled Faith even tighter into his embrace. His first instinct was to keep her safe. He looked around again. No one seemed out of place. He didn't even see the dark hair; most of the heads were wearing hats. He reasoned with himself it was just nerves. He shook it off and released Faith, not wanting to make her parents think he was the kind of man to put on an embarrassing show of PDA.

"Ryan? Is something wrong?"

"Wait a minute…"

Faith suddenly pulled her phone out of her clear bag and looked at it. First, she seemed annoyed, then puzzled, and then he saw fear in her eyes. She quickly stuffed the phone back into her bag with a resolute expression.

"What's wrong," he asked her.

"Another weird call, actually a text. It was from a number I didn't recognize. The text said, 'ENJOYING THE GAME?' Is he here? How does he know where I am?" she looked around for someone, but she didn't know exactly who.

"Don't erase that text. I'll have Doyle investigate it when we get back to Tulsa. I can't do anything about it right now."

"I-I'm ok-kay."

"I also thought I saw someone out of place. I'm not sure we're safe here. We should leave; I'll take you home. You'll be safe with me."

"I'm tired of being afraid. My parents are here. You're here. I will be okay."

"We're safer in public. Just stay close to me."

"Should we tell Mom and Dad?"

"I'll tell them."

Ryan informed Carolyn and Luther of what was happening. They were worried. He assured them that he had a handle on the situation.

The rest of the game was spent with all of them on high alert. Ryan was in cop mode. He kept his arm around Faith until it was time to go. When the game was over, the Sooners won. The celebration was wild.

They waited for the crowd to thin enough so that there was no chance they could be separated. As they left the stadium, he clutched Faith's hand in his, and his arm linked through hers. He kept the group ambling for the two-mile hike to their cars. He'd told them to act nonchalantly as if they weren't being hunted. He kept his eyes roving the crowds, looking for a threat.

When they arrived at their rides, they said goodbye. He reminded them to drive safely and call when they got home.

On the way home, Ryan carefully took the long way, adding unnecessary turns and exits. He kept an eye out behind him. He didn't want to be followed.

When he arrived at Faith's apartment, he went inside with her and checked the rooms to ensure they were clear.

"I can stay here tonight."

"I'll be okay."

"Faith, I can stay on the couch. I will stay anyway, either out in my car all night or here."

"Ryan, I'll be alright."

"Please, I'll call Evon to come over…"

"I don't know."

"I just want to keep you safe."

"Maybe… I haven't been getting much sleep anyway. We can call Evon, and I'll stay up with you."

Evon came over quickly, and the three of them talked. They tried to keep the conversation light and casual. As it got later, the two women were running out of steam. Ryan stayed vigilant.

After four am, Evon and Faith finally fell asleep. Faith was on the couch, with her head on his shoulder. Her long, dark hair covered her face and trailed down his arm. He was still on alert, but his mind was wandering. He was being ridiculous. He scared Faith because he thought someone was watching him and overreacted. So far, there wasn't even a glimpse or a sound of anyone or anything out of place. He prayed for peace and guidance. As dawn came, he finally succumbed to sleep.

A smile spread across his face as he watched Faith's apartment from his vantage point in the house across the street. He could see into her kitchen from his top-story bedroom window. Her curtains were open, and he could see her as she washed the dishes, unaware. He was biding his time.

He had slowly revealed himself to Faith. He could see that she was agitated because she was washing and rewashing the same dish over and over. She was biting the inside of her lower lip, a gesture of her unease. He could see her clenching her jaw.

He knew he had rattled her and intimidated her guardian, too. That message he had sent put them both on edge. It had been all he could do to stifle his vomit when they kissed. In fact, after sending the text, he escaped down the tunnel to the bathroom and was violently sick. Now, they both knew he was watching them.

Ashley had also told him Faith was a nervous wreck. She was angry that Faith was asking questions about him. She was afraid that Faith would try to break them up. She would go ballistic if she knew the truth; she already hated Faith. He didn't know if it was jealousy because of the policeman- Ryan or something else. But he didn't care; he only cared about getting Faith back.

Ashley didn't realize that he was slowly transforming her into Faith. He'd convinced her that she would be lovely with dark hair. He'd gotten her to get brown contacts; he told her that she was beautiful.

He chuckled; Ashley was so clueless that she couldn't see what he was doing. He was even buying her outfits that were like something he would have bought Faith to wear. One day, both women wore the same outfit; Ashley had been furious at first and then gloated because she thought Faith was trying to be more like her.

Ashley would never be Faith, only a pale facsimile. But he could pretend she was with the changes he'd made in her. He groaned as he thought about Faith. He missed her so much that it physically hurt. He could use the new, improved Ashley to ease the ever-present pain. It wasn't love, and it never would even be affection. His heart belonged to only one woman: Faith.

He was feeling desperate. He needed Faith. Without her, nothing in his world was right. A hole in his soul ached when they weren't together. Life was difficult without her in it. Everything was meaningless. Everyday life seemed empty and unending. It was an unbroken line of misery.

But it wouldn't be long before he came out of the shadows and claimed her for his own. His plans were falling into place. He picked up his phone and dialed the number... Soon, My Love, soon.

Chapter 15

Faith was absentmindedly washing the dishes in her tiny, beige kitchenette, and her thoughts went to Ryan. That was happening more than it should. She realized she had spent most of her free time with Ryan. They'd not kissed again, but he gave great hugs. Sometimes, when he hugged her, she felt like he was putting the broken pieces of her heart together.

She was falling for him. That wasn't good because he'd told her he didn't want to date a woman seriously. She'd initially agreed because of her bad experience with Charles, but she was finding out that Ryan was different. She wished she could make him see that they might have something special.

Her main problem was the phone calls and the notes. Every day, she got a strange message or a strange call. Each of them ended with 'See you soon, My Love.' It was very unsettling. She'd told Ryan, and he told her he was watching it. He'd even gotten Maggie's son Doyle in on the investigation. There was just no way to trace the messages.

She started daydreaming as she tidied up. Ryan was coming over tonight with Doyle and Ellie; she let her thoughts wander to him. What she had with Ryan was beautiful, whatever it was. She wanted her future to include Ryan. But in what way? Faith was starting to dream about forever. She shook the idea out of her head. She wouldn't go after the stars; God had given her Ryan for the present. She wouldn't second guess God's timing. But she thought it would be divine if Ryan would get more serious about her.

Her phone rang, and she saw an unknown number. Probably spam.

"Hello?"

Faith heard heavy breathing on the other end of the call.

"Hello? Can I help you?" she used the fake voice she greeted telemarketers with.

"Faith… Faith…" the distorted voice said her name, and then there was more heavy breathing.

"Can I help you?"

"Faith..."

"Sorry, I'm not interested." Stupid robocalls.

Before she could end the call, the Voice breathed, "Have patience, Faith… I'll be seeing you… soon, My Love."

Faith hung up instantly. That had been unsettling. It wasn't a typical telemarketing call. She shook it off. Her imagination was getting the best of her. With a prayer, she returned her mind to her task. She started scrubbing the pots with a vengeance.

She should tell Ryan. He needed to know if her mystery caller was now calling her cell number. He would know what to do. She dialed the phone.

"R-Ryan?" her voice sounded panicked in her ears.

"Yes?"

"I-I-I got another call at home on my cellphone."

Instantly, he sounded all business, "What did they say?"

She felt like an idiot.

"It seemed to be a sales call. But it was that same auto-tuned voice. It called my name, and when I said I wasn't interested, it said, "I'll be seeing you soon, my Love."

"Are you okay?"

"I don't know. Whoever it is knows my name. And why say "my Love?" That can't be normal."

"Maybe it's just a sales call?"

"Ryan, I'm afraid. Charles always contacted me after I broke up with him and left. It didn't matter if I changed my number or moved. He always found me. He wanted me to know that he would always find me. All these calls, saying My Love, now they know my name? I know it can't be a coincidence. He knows my number!"

"I will keep you safe," he vowed.

"Thank you, Ryan. I know you will try. But Ryan, he always finds me."

"If he does, he'll have to deal with me."

"He was so violent. I don't want you or anyone else to get hurt."

"I'm a cop and a good one. Don't be afraid. Besides, I was already coming over. Ellie and Doyle will be there too. I'll be there soon. We'll have a good night, don't be afraid."

Ryan ended the call. His jaw clenched. He was troubled. He wanted to keep her safe. All these strange things kept happening to her. He tried to get to the bottom of it. He would follow up on any leads. Everything was just so weird. The calls she'd been getting at school were strange. This call had obviously upset her. With a psycho possibly on her tail, he should take the strange things seriously. He had experienced some of the strange occurrences. He'd had the strange vehicle follow him. He was supposed to keep her safe; he had an obligation as a cop, but also because he was starting to care about her. But did she feel the same way?

They had been spending lots of time together. They hadn't kissed again, not that he didn't want to. He had been trying to keep things on the surface between them. After his mistakes with Ashley, he was going to take his time. He didn't want to make the same ones with Faith.

His eyes fell on a picture of his mother. She was smiling. He would have loved for his mom to meet Faith. She would've loved Faith. His mom would probably tell him to stay with her and not let her go. His mom would want him to date her seriously.

He thought that if his mom had lived, maybe he would be a different kind of man. It had been easier to trust God with his mom to talk to. Maggie had done her best to fill in and always warned him that he needed to change his ways or that the right one would get away. He used to laugh that off. Ryan wondered if he would laugh if he and Faith ended things. He wondered what his mom would think if he were to lose Faith. He had a hard time thinking of the future without her.

But now, he was learning to trust the Lord again. He needed to give his relationship with Faith to God. He prayed.

"God, please guide me. I don't know what to do about Faith. I care about her, but I'm worried about her and whoever is bothering her. Help me keep her safe."

He felt at peace when he was done praying. God would show him what to do with Faith.

Chapter 16

Faith hummed to herself as she cut out the folder games for her class; she was happy. Well, most of the time, how could she help it? She pictured Ryan's blue eyes and his smile.

She set down her scissors. Was Ryan happy with their relationship, whatever it was? She wrinkled her forehead in a slight frown. She didn't want to get too attached; what if he didn't want a serious relationship with her? She was finding herself wishing they could be together. He hadn't kissed her again. Why? Did he just want to be friends? She wasn't sure she would be happy with that anymore. It wasn't good.

The school day was over, and she put the games she was making away and gathered her things. She'd waited long enough, and it was time to go home. Faith was feeling disappointed and a little nervous. Ryan hadn't been able to walk her to her car that day. He had a meeting with his captain about some vandalism at the school. She was angry with herself. She was weak. She shouldn't rely only on Ryan. She should be courageous in the Lord. She said a quick prayer for courage, and juggling several bags, she walked to her car.

She stopped and stared at her car's windshield. There was a note. Charles had left many messages on her car, in her car, and inside the rooms she lived in after the breakup. Now, here was another one. She dropped her bags. Her hands shook when she reached for it. She kept telling herself that she was in the shadow of the Almighty. She would be safe.

Faith took the note and opened it. There's nothing scary there, just a coupon for her favorite sandwich shop. The shop she and Ryan had gone to on their date the day she met him. She had told Kat, Angel, and Ashley yesterday that she had been craving a Philly cheese steak sandwich from that specific restaurant. She quickly glanced at the other cars in the parking lot. None of the other vehicles had flyers on their windshields. That was odd and a little creepy.

She thought of stopping there for dinner. Using the coupon would make it less menacing. She told herself that it would quickly put her fears at rest to go there and get a sandwich and eat it there. She considered calling Ryan and asking him to meet her there after his meeting. She thought about asking Evon, but she wanted to prove to herself that she wasn't a scared little wimp. She would not be weak. She told herself she wasn't going to give in to fear. Besides, she wanted a Philly cheese steak sandwich, she reasoned.

Faith walked into the little hole-in-the-wall restaurant. She quickly looked around. Nothing was scary inside. She felt like a fool. How ridiculous to have gotten so worked up over something innocent. She had to stop jumping at shadows.

After getting her order and heading to a table, she saw a man walk in.

The man had black hair, dark eyes, glasses, a short goatee, and a mustache. It was the man from the café. Something about him made her shiver. He didn't speak to her, but he stared at her.

She sat down shakily. She tried to ignore him. She tried to eat. He watched every bite she took. It was unnerving. The man was so much like Charles that she felt a scream rising in her throat—the same bone structure but leaner. The similarities were uncanny. She lost her appetite. Wrapping her sandwich in its paper, she got up to leave. She would have to pass the man to get to the door. Faith tried to take a deep, calming belly breath and walked past him without glancing at him.

She felt cold in the pit of her stomach, and hot tears were stinging behind her eyes. Her mouth went dry. She felt her breath coming faster and faster; she couldn't get a deep breath. She broke out in a cold sweat. What was wrong with her? Was she having a panic attack? She was afraid she couldn't drive and had to escape that man. Only one thing came to mind: she needed to call Ryan. He would know what to do.

Faith practically ran to her car. She was locking herself in as quickly as she could. She tried to steady her breathing.

Then she called Ryan's number. It rang once, twice; she was about to hang up when Ryan answered.

"Hey! Faith, what can I do for you?"

"I- I- I was j-ju- just having d-di- din- dinner," she couldn't control her breathing, and her voice sounded strained in her ears.

"Faith? Is everything okay?"

She wanted to tell him she was fine and just wanted to clear up something about school, but all that came out was a wail and storm of tears.

"Faith, you're scaring me. Are you all right? Do you need help?"

"I'm having a panic attack. I'm a bit afraid to drive home. I can't stop crying," she hated sounding weak and helpless. She needed to pray.

"Pray with me, please, Ryan. I can't calm down."

"I will."

"I'm so scared, Ryan, I don't have the words."

"Dear God, send your peace to surround Faith. Keep her safe."

"Thank you."

"Do you need me to come to get you?" his voice was genuinely worried.

"I think that might be a good idea. I'm sorry. I don't usually fall apart like this," she said, burning with embarrassment, which didn't help her get calmer.

"It's okay. Where are you?"

"At Steak Stuffers."

"Try and calm down; I'm on my way," he sounded reassuring.

"Please keep praying for me."

"I will."

Faith sat in her locked car and tried every strategy she knew to help herself calm down. She kept a prayer in her heart.

He was still watching. She kept telling herself he wasn't Charles; he may resemble him, but Charles was still in Texas. She pictured Charles' beach blonde hair and green eyes. This man couldn't be Charles.

Just as she was starting to feel her heartbeat slow, the man smiled at her in an oddly familiar, twisted smile, got up, walked out of the restaurant, and stalked past her car, never taking his eyes off hers until he walked off down the street. She took a deep breath and let the tears come.

When Ryan arrived, she was in control again, barely. He insisted on driving her home. On the way, she told him about the man. Any fear that he would laugh was put to rest with his attentive nods and glances. He was in cop mode.

"We can get footage of the parking lot," he suggested.

As he talked to her, she felt relaxed. She was starting to smile again when he had her home. He called an Uber to ride him to his bike. They sat on her small blue sofa while he waited for his ride-share. She told him more about how Charles had hounded her after the breakup.

"He followed me everywhere. I couldn't get away from him. There were notes every day, everywhere. He made sure I understood that he knew my every move."

"Knowing that, why did you go to Steak Stuffers alone? You should have asked me to come with you." He was no-nonsense, "I can't keep you safe if you deliberately put yourself in harm's way."

"I'm tired of being weak. I'm tired of living in fear. I take every precaution I can. I don't want to be this way. I'm trying to trust in God."

"Faith, you're not weak. It's okay to need help. I can't keep you safe if you keep me in the dark. Don't you trust me?"

"I do. I just want to be brave."

"I know you are brave. You're strong. Everyday. I watch you. I know. I admire your strength,"

"It feels weak to rely so much on you. I don't want to need you."

"Did you ever think that I need to keep you safe? I need you to be safe," he tilted her face to look up at him.

"That's just your cop ego talking."

"No Faith. It's more than that," she thought he might kiss her, and her heart sped up.

"Ryan, I… I'll ask for help next time. I just hate needing it."

"We all need help sometimes. This is something out of your control."

"That's what I hate. I used to be in control. Charles took that from me."

"You've taught me to let God control the things that are out of your hands. But He has put you in my path. I can help keep you safe. But you have to be smart. Let me help you."

"Okay, Ryan, you win. No more heroics. I'll lean on God and you."

"Thank you," he switched to cop mode, "I'll talk to Dr. A about seeing that parking lot footage. I'll get to the bottom of this."

"Thank you."

He changed modes on a dime, suddenly wrapped her in his strong arms, and kissed her softly on her head. She felt some of his strength seeping into her as he held her. It was a balm on her stinging heart.

"My Uber is here. Be safe."

"You too!"

His pulse beat faster, and he thought his heart might explode. He was on property across from her shabby apartment, waiting for her. Today was the day he had been preparing for for months. She would be his, finally. He would reveal himself to her. His patience had finally paid off. He could almost feel her in his arms and taste her kisses.

He had found out where she lived many months ago. He had been there many times, watching and planning. He had seen them together too often. Faith hadn't betrayed him completely. She hadn't kissed the policeman again. They had embraced, yes, but Faith was loyal to him. He knew she was missing him, wanting him as much as he missed and wanted her. He knew she was thinking of him.

Every time he had been near her, he could see that he was haunting her, the way she haunted him. He had even come to her classroom, seeing her so close that he could smell the soft vanilla scent she wore. It had been such exquisite torture to be near her.

Even though it had made his stomach clench in pain, he would watch her spend time with Ryan. He thought she must know he was watching, and she was jealous and unhappy without him, and this other... man was just a cry for him to return to her. Well, he would come back- and with a vengeance.

He knew he was in her head and would be in her arms tonight. He was counting the seconds till she would be home, alone, waiting for him.

He knew what he had to do. She would be so happy to see him. Besides, she had seen him with Ashley- she hadn't recognized him, but she knew it was him- she would be jealous. That would teach her to carry on with that other... man, what was good for the goose was good for the gander. She had been a flirt and a tease with him- but he had stopped that behavior once before. He loved her too much to let her get away with that. After he had her back in his arms, then he would teach her a lesson she wouldn't forget. He would make sure another man never tempted her again.

He would take her away with him tonight, and they could return to their idyllic life together- forever.

Chapter 17

Faith smiled as she thought about Ryan walking her to her car every day. It made her feel special and important. The strange papers appeared there more often, but Ryan cared about her security.

Now, it was every day that she found something waiting, slipped under the windshield wipers. It was unnerving. No one else seemed to be getting the flyers and coupons. There were never any notes, just those strange papers waiting for her every day after school. Charles had always left her messages on her car; he had never been this subtle. She asked Dr. Abernathy about the parking lot camera, but it seemed to stay on the fritz.

That thought wiped the smile from her face. She continued to see that strange, menacing man all around the town. He must have been Ashley's boyfriend; she had even seen him at the school. Once, he had come with Ashley to her classroom. He was so like Charles, but there were differences. The close-clipped beard and mustache seemed to mask him. His eyes, framed by glasses, were dark, not green. His hair was also black, not blonde. Strangely, he never spoke. Ashley was always dominating the conversation; he never got a word in. Faith wished he would talk; hearing his voice would put Charles' ghost to rest.

The day Ashley brought him to her classroom, Faith told Ryan about how nervous the man made her. Now Ryan stayed with her after school. It seemed to make Ashley even angrier with her.

Ashley had also been acting strangely. She'd started to resemble Faith as best she could. She didn't seem to realize it either. Ashley would mimic her hairstyles. They even showed up to school in the same outfit. Faith asked her about it, and she preened and said the new look was Charlie's idea. When Faith tried asking her about her boyfriend, Ashley got angry and disagreeable. She would tell Faith to keep out of her relationship with Charlie.

But it seemed Charlie was everywhere she went, mainly with Ashley. She felt like he was following her like Charles used to do. Could he be Charles? She was trying to convince herself he wasn't. She felt like she was always looking over her shoulder for him. She felt safest with Ryan.

Faith was excitedly straightening the living room and kitchen. Ryan was coming over tonight around five o'clock. They would hang out until it was time to go to Maggie's for dinner at six. She decided to take a quick nap when the rooms were in order. She hadn't been sleeping well. She was so tired that sleep came swiftly, and soon she was out.

The sound of knocking intruded into her restless dreams. Faith nearly jumped, and she fell off the couch. Her face was wet with tears when she realized the knocking was coming from the door. She shook off the bad dream. Curse these nightmares; not even a nap was safe. She was too anxious, and it was just Ryan, after all. She called, "I'm coming, Ryan!" as she unlocked the door. She was so keyed up that she didn't look out the peephole like usual. There were three extra locks and a deadbolt.

As soon as she opened the door, a hand grabbed hers, and she looked up into the emerald-green eyes of Charles Meredith. She screamed. He pulled her hard to his chest; he shut the door before she could punch him. His face was clean-shaven again, but his hair was still dark and slicked to his head, but she would know those green eyes anywhere.

"Faith! My Love!" he cried, clutching her tightly.

"Ch- Ch- Charles?" she screamed and tried to pull away.

"Now, Faith! Why would you behave like that? Didn't you miss me?" he crooned, pulling her deeper into his arms. He began to kiss her.

"Miss you?" Faith was terrified as she jerked her head away from his kisses; he had found her here. She *had* been seeing him; he was Charlie Meridian. He had been responsible for the notes. All those things that had made her uneasy- he was here. He'd been here for months!

"I've missed you. You know how much I need you, how much you need me."

"I don't need you," she squeaked as fear took hold of her, and her heart cried out a prayer for safety.

"You mean you have someone else? You must be talking about… Officer Ryan, was it?"

"Ryan, he's a, a, a friend, a good friend, and…" she cut herself short; it would be better if Charles didn't know Ryan was coming over tonight.

"He is the Campus Rent-a-Cop I saw today when I went by your school. What am I going to do with you, Faith? I've been so patient. I've been talking to a charming teacher friend of yours, Ashley Sheridan. She thinks we're dating. Of course, I'm only seeing her to get closer to you. She said you had been making a fool of yourself over that cop, Ryan Madsen. Faith, you don't have to try to make me jealous. You know I don't love her; I still love only you. You are still mine."

"Never again!" she shouted.

She elbowed him in the chest, freeing herself for a fraction of a second. Faith ran across the room in a panic, and he grabbed her in a flash effortlessly. She tried to find a way to escape him again, squirming and wriggling; it only excited him, and she could feel his rapid heartbeat against her chest. Then he dragged her to her couch as she kicked him with all her might, but he didn't flinch and pulled her more tightly into his embrace.

"Faith! So, you want to play?" His smile was wicked and delighted as he kissed her, his lips holding her prisoner.

She couldn't get away.

Then the Scripture came to her, "I will say concerning the LORD, who is my refuge and my fortress, my God in whom I trust: He Himself will rescue you…." God would keep her safe.

Ryan was finger-combing his hair as he looked in the mirror. Tonight should be a great night. He would be spending it with his two favorite women. Ryan was thinking more and more about seriously dating Faith. He might as well be dating her now. Why not make it official? If he could be sure what he was feeling was real. He didn't want to make another mistake; he especially didn't want to hurt Faith. She had been hurt so much. She should be happy.

While he adjusted his belt, he pondered what a relationship with Faith might look like. He could easily picture her sitting in his breakfast nook, sharing a meal with him. He could see her curled up on his oversized plaid couch next to him, watching TV together. He let himself remember those kisses. But was that enough?

What if something happened to her? What if her ex-fiancé showed up and hurt her? What if he lost her? Was opening himself up to that kind of pain worth it?

Ryan shook off the unpleasant thoughts, grabbed his keys, and went to his red Toyota truck. He would pick up Faith and go to Maggie's together. It promised to be a great night.

As Ryan drove down the road to Faith's apartment building, he had a gnawing feeling of unease growing in his gut. He knew that something was wrong. That still, small voice he was learning to listen to told him to get to Faith's as fast as possible down the road. He never hit a red light once.

When he got to Faith's apartment complex, he hopped out of his truck and looked around. What could be wrong? He picked up his phone and called her. It rang and rang, but she didn't pick up. Now, he was very concerned. Then he saw the dark sedan. It looked just like the one that had followed him. He told himself that Tulsa had hundreds of dark sedans. He couldn't be sure it was the same. But the feeling of danger grew. He looked up toward Faith's apartment and saw something through the window. He could see a man with Faith in his arms!   Then he heard Faith shout.

Faith's phone started to ring. Could it be Ryan? What if he was calling to say he couldn't come? She would be utterly helpless. Charles wrapped her tighter in his arms.

"Let it ring; nothing will disturb us tonight. You're all mine. We must get you ready to go; you're coming home with me."

"B-b- but Charles, I can't go… I have to work tomorrow."

"You'll never have to work again. I'll take care of you. Just you and me, my Love."

"Charles, I won't go with you."

"Yes, you will," he growled, "I'm a patient man, but you have pushed me too far. I don't want to hurt you, but we're leaving together- tonight."

"Never!" she shouted at the top of her lungs, desperately hoping someone would hear her.

She felt his slap sting across her face so hard her eyes filled with tears.

"See what you made me do?" he hissed, then smashed his lips into hers.

Faith's anguished shout hit Ryan like a lightning bolt- he loved her. However, this was not the time for that; she needed a cop, not a lover. He instantly thought of her ex. Could the man in the window be the same? This man didn't match Faith's description, but he would bet his next paycheck that it was the same man.

Ryan got his cell phone and called the dispatcher. He told them all about the situation as much as he could tell. That was done. He decided to see if he could do anything to help. He felt for his gun in its holster. He would have to be cautious; Faith could get hurt if he was too rash. He would play it cool and try to get in there with her. His heart prayed for her safety and the wisdom to help her. "God, please keep her safe! Help me know what to do to keep her safe!"

Then he went carefully up the stairs to her apartment.

"Knock, knock," the familiar voice said in accompaniment with his knocks on the door, "Faith? It's Ryan; remember I'm taking you to Maggie's tonight?"

Charles reluctantly pulled his lips from hers. Then he smiled and signaled for her to open the door. Faith looked straight into his eyes and scrubbed his kiss from her lips into her sleeve. Then, she tried to yell out the door for Ryan to get help. Charles seemed to know what she was planning to do. He grabbed her and clamped his hand across her mouth.

"Ha, ha, ha, please excuse us a minute, Ryan, was it?" Charles said as he opened the door, inadvertently releasing Faith. "You must excuse Faith. I surprised her with a visit. She and I were engaged; there was a silly little mishap, and she ran away here, but now I'm back, and we're getting back together. I'm Charles Meredith; surely, you've heard of me."

Ryan looked at her, then smiled his big smile, but it wasn't as warm as it usually was. This time, it was fierce. Faith tried to signal him to leave, but he barely shook his head. She went cautiously to the arm of the oversized brown leather couch. What was Ryan planning?

"Wow, Faith," Ryan said, "You told me that your ex- sorry Charles- that your fiancé was one of those bleach blonde types. Did you get a new look, Charles, was it?" he had met this man before, in one of Ashley's attempts to shove her new boyfriend in his face, she had introduced him as Charlie Meridian, the guy she had been seeing since around the time school got started. He went and sat at the opposite end of the brown couch.

"Are you also Charlie Meridian? You look a lot like this guy our friend Ashley is dating."

"I was spending time with her, but Faith is, and always will be, *my* girl."

"Ryan, Charles is back. He wants me to go with him. Tonight." Faith's eyes were full of tears, and she was trying to keep them from falling. Why wouldn't Ryan shoot him or get help or something? She thought maybe he didn't care that much for me. If he could sit there like that while Charles was here, he didn't care.

"Faith, you know I would never stand in the path of true love. Just accept my congratulations, you two. Charles, you don't mind if I give my friend here a little hug to congratulate her, do you?" Ryan said while coming closer, inch by inch, to where Faith sat still as a statue on the arm of the couch. Then he quickly pulled her into his arms and held her tight, "Congratulations, Faith!" like lightning, he bent his head and whispered, "The police are on their way; I'm not leaving you."

"Oh, Ryan! You always were such a good friend." She understood. Ryan was playing along till help could arrive. She was safe. Ryan wouldn't let Charles take her. They just needed to keep Charles calm until the police could arrive. She beamed at him; the actor inside her rose to the occasion, "You know Charles, that this sweet guy, he has been just like a brother to me." She had to convince Charles that Ryan wasn't a threat.

"Ryan, it's good to know my Love has such a good friend." Charles came over, took Faith's hand, and returned her to his arms.

Ryan held her tighter for a moment, so she gave him the slightest of winks. She could feel the tension in his arms as he let Charles pull her forcefully into his.

"Well, since my two boys are here together, I couldn't be happier!"

Charles looked at both, and his lips made an oily, greasy, slimy bow that was somehow meant to be a smile.

"Faith, my Love. You don't think I am that stupid, do you? I told you I've been 'seeing' that very chatty teacher friend of yours. I know everything you do. You can stop this charade; I know the two of you have been dating," he was menacing.

"We're just friends!" She had to convince Charles that Ryan was just a friend; that's all they were.

"Then why are you spending all your time with him? I've even seen you kiss him."

"You saw that? That was weeks ago!"

"I've been extremely patient with you. Now it's time to come with me."

She stiffened in Charles' embrace. "What? Now?"

"Where are you taking her?"

"I have a place. Why would I tell you? You'll never find her."

"Charles, I'm not ready. I- I- I must pack." She stalled. She needed to find a way to keep him here. If he tried to leave with her, Ryan would stop him, and Ryan might get hurt. Charles often became violent quickly.

"I have everything ready for you there; you won't need anything."

"Charles, please let me at least get my toothbrush."

"My Love, I'm afraid I can't trust you out of my sight. Ryan, it's time for you to go. We don't need you." Charles glared at him, "Isn't that right, my Love?" Then Charles quickly wrapped his arms around hers like a vice and kissed her passionately on the mouth. Faith was trying not to gag.

Ryan was nearly at the end of his endurance, seeing her valiant smile and frightened eyes. Now Charles had her again and was kissing her, and he couldn't think of any way to get her back safe with him in his arms. Seeing Charles' lips on Faith's was about to put him over the edge; his arms longed to hold her. He wasn't jealous- he knew Faith didn't love Charles. He hated to admit it because he was a cop, but watching the other man holding the woman he loved scared him. He couldn't let Charles take her. His hand hovered above his concealed holster. If Charles tried to leave with Faith, he would shoot him.

The doorbell rang, and a knock came at the door.

"Who is that? Another boyfriend?" Charles' voice was icy.

"Tulsa PD, open up, please."

When the police shouted, Charles released her and growled, "This isn't over! You are mine." Then he took off.

"In here!" Ryan shouted as he flew to the door.

When the locks were undone, and before his fellow officers were inside, he grabbed Faith and held her as if she were his lifeline.

By the time the officer came in, Charles was gone. He had jumped out of the back window, breaking it. Faith was still in Ryan's arms, and he wasn't letting go. Doyle was there and checked the apartment, ensuring that Charles wasn't hiding somewhere. Ryan brought Faith to the brown couch, which for once wasn't covered in clean laundry; she was shaking. He was reluctant to let go of her as if she could vanish if he did. He sat her on the couch and rubbed her shoulders.

"Are you okay, Faith?" he asked her.

"I think I'm going to be sick," she got up and ran to the restroom.

"I'll get you some water," he said, entering the kitchen. When he got there, he felt himself let go. He breathed several times deeply and shook it off. She was safe. He hadn't lost her. He breathed a thankful prayer that God helped him get here in time. If Charles had taken her… he couldn't finish the thought. He loved her, and he knew it now. He took a deep, cleansing breath, got a big bottle of water from the fridge, and brought it to the couch.

"Faith, can I help you?"

"I'm all right."

She came back looking peaked and pale and sat on the couch. Doyle came over to where they sat.

"I need to know everything," Doyle said.

She explained what had happened that afternoon. Then she began telling them about her past with Charles.

"He was abusive. He'd hit me. He was careful about it. No one ever saw the bruises. I never told anyone. Not till I left him. No one would believe me. He had connections. Once, a motel manager called the police. Charles paid off the motel, and the manager told the police not to come. That was the night he brought me back to his apartment. For once, I put up a fight. A neighbor called, and the police came out to check on it. I got away from him, and I never looked back. I don't know if the police followed up or if he got in trouble. I stayed in a women's shelter for a few days. They wanted me to press charges, but I was too afraid. So, I left. All I cared about was getting away. That's when I left Texas. I lived with my parents in Antlers, a small town in Southeastern Oklahoma, for a year. Then I moved here. I hoped I'd lost him. But I was afraid he'd find me. He did. I'll never be safe."

Her story explained so much. She had been abused. He vowed that if he could win her, he would do his best to keep her safe and happy.

He came to the couch where she was sitting. He sat next to her and took her hand. He was gently rubbing circles on the top of it. He scooted next to her and wrapped his arm around her. She didn't pull away. She nestled into his side. He squeezed her shoulders tighter. He didn't want to let go. She looked so small, and there were still tears in her eyes. Her eyes darted around the room, lingering on the door. Then she shivered. He took the burgundy throw blanket off the back of the couch and wrapped it around her. She smiled a trembling, grateful smile.

"Ryan, thank you. I wouldn't be here if you'd not come."

"Don't be afraid. I made it in time. Thank God!"

When they were done searching and got all the information they could, the police started leaving. Doyle came to where the two of them sat on the couch.

"Don't stay here tonight," Doyle told her, "Go somewhere else. Preferably somewhere you've never stayed before."

"I can get a room somewhere."

"No, you won't, Faith," Ryan was stern.

"I'm taking you somewhere where I can keep you safe. Somewhere, I can keep both eyes on you." He thought about it and then had an idea, "I've got it! Faith, you are staying with me tonight. I won't take no for an answer. It's the only way I can be sure you're safe. Please don't fight me on this."

"Ryan, I can't stay with you. I can stay at a hotel tonight."

"Faith, do it for my sake. I'll be useless if I don't know you're safe with me. Please?"

"I know. Why don't you call Mom?" Doyle suggested.

"Ryan! Maggie must be worried; we were going to her place to have dinner."

"I'll call her," Ryan said.

Maggie answered on the first ring.

"Ryan! What's happened to you and Faith? Did you forget dinner?"

"No, Maggie. Something, rather someone, came up."

"Well, tell me… I don't need a mystery."

"Faith's ex-fiancé, Charles, showed up at her apartment."

"Oh no! Is Faith all right?"

"She'll be okay. I showed up before he could take her with him. I called the cops- Doyle's here- when they showed up, Charles left. The guys have been looking for him but haven't found him yet."

"Praise God you got there in time, Ryan!"

"Maggie, Doyle says she can't stay in her apartment. He wants her to stay somewhere else. Talk some sense to her. Tell her to stay at my place."

"Ryan, why can't she stay with me?"

"I need to be able to keep an eye on her."

"You stay here too. You know I've got the room. Let me talk to her."

Ryan handed his phone to Faith and put it on speaker mode.

"Faith? Honey! Come and stay with me."

"Maggie. I can't put you in danger. Charles is sure to find me again."

"The police want you out of there."

"I can stay at a motel."

"No, you're staying with me. Ryan will stay with us. He'll keep us safe."

"But what if Charles comes? He might hurt you."

"That's why Ryan will stay with us."

"I don't want him to get hurt either."

"God will keep us safe. Trust in the Lord. I'm not taking no for an answer. Ask Doyle and Ryan. They know not to cross me."

Faith looked at both men.

"Please, Faith, at least stay with Maggie. I need to be able to keep you safe." Ryan gave her his patented puppy dog eyes.

"Are you sure?" Faith asked Maggie.

"I insist." Maggie was firm.

"Okay. We'll be over soon. I've got to pack a bag."

"I'll see you. Be safe. Listen to my boys."

"I will." Faith had the ghost of a smile on her lips.

Ryan took back his phone.

"Thank you, Maggie. I feel better knowing I can keep her safe."

When he ended the call, he asked Faith, "Can I help you pack?"

"I- I -I just don't know what I'll need. I'm a little rattled."

"You get your clothes, and I'll get your toiletries if you don't mind. You wouldn't want me to pick out your clothes. But I do like that red dress you wore Sunday."

"Thank you," Faith gave a giggle that ended in a sob.

"You've got this. You've been so brave; don't wimp out on me now."

"You'd better let me pack myself. Can you collect my school bag and my tablet?"

"Got it."

She managed to get a bag packed. Ryan had all her school things. He led her out to the parking lot.

"We'll take my truck. I haven't used it much this year. Hopefully, Charles won't recognize it."

"I can't ever thank you enough for calling the police, for staying with me till they came. I can't think about what would happen if you hadn't been here. When you came, I wasn't as scared. Ryan, I'm sorry I dragged you into this," her eyes glistened with unshed tears.

"Stop. I knew what was going on when I came up to your apartment. I heard your scream. I jumped into it. I would do it again."

"I believe God has put you in my life for a reason. I knew you would keep me safe."

"I will always keep you safe." He vowed.

Chapter 18

Ryan drove them to Maggie's house. Maggie was waiting for them at the door. When Faith got out of the truck, Maggie held her arms out. Faith stepped into her warm and welcoming hug.

"Faith, I'm so glad you're still with us."

"Thanks to Ryan and his quick thinking," she looked over her shoulder at the strong, handsome man carrying her bag.

"I've kept dinner warm for y'all, Honey."

"Thank you. I feel terrible about staying here- putting you in danger. I'd never forgive myself if something were to happen to you."

"Let's trust God. Besides, Ryan will be here. I know he will do whatever it takes to keep us safe."

"I've been trying to trust the Lord but feel so vulnerable and scared."

"That is perfectly natural. You've been through an ordeal. I can't imagine the fear you felt. You're safe now, Ryan's here, and Doyle has some cops keeping watch on the place."

Faith could feel the stinging of tears threatening to spill. Maggie would think she was ungrateful. She had to pull herself together. She could still see Charles' green eyes looking into hers. The crazed look of desperation and evil seared into her memory. Had he become even more psychotic since she'd escaped him in

Texas? His voice was full of anger and pain as he'd vowed to take her away.

"Faith? Do you need a minute to freshen up? Use the bathroom on the second floor; I'll have Ryan take your things to the upstairs bedroom on the left."

"Yes, thank you. I do need a minute," she tried not to run to the bathroom.

When she got there, she fell apart. All the feelings of fear, guilt, and shame washed over her. She felt responsible. Charles wouldn't be in her life if she had made better choices. All the fears that she had locked up tight came flooding over her.

He was here. He'd found her. He still wanted her. He was still violent and desperate. If that was love, she wanted no part of it.

Faith shook herself. God's love wasn't like that. God's love was perfect. If only Ryan could love like that. But Ryan had made it clear he didn't want a serious relationship. She needed to slow down. She shouldn't rely so much on Ryan. He would let her down. Could anyone love her? She wished Ryan could. But she needed to let that go. Now that he had seen how dangerous her life was, how she had brought someone like Charles into it, he would want no part of her. She realized that she did want love, the healthy kind, the kind of love God wanted a man to have for a woman. More than that, she wanted it specifically from Ryan. She was in love with him.

Faith was crying. Ugly crying. Her mascara had run, and she was pale, except for her red eyes. Her nose was blotchy and running. She knew she must look frightening, but her emotions were so overwhelming that she couldn't care.

She stood at the sink, letting go. She didn't hear footsteps outside the door. She barely registered the light tap on the door frame. She hadn't shut the door and suddenly felt arms enfolding her.

She jerked to attention. A flash of fear passed through her. But this embrace was so gentle that her fear dissipated. Ryan.

"Faith, I'm sorry, I shouldn't bother you, but Maggie has dinner ready."

She turned in his arms, and he pulled her into his chest.

"Faith…" he murmured, cradling her softly, "You're safe now."

"Ryan…"

"Hush now, everything is going to be all right now. I'm here."

His words made her feel conflicted. She felt safe with him but needed to stop relying on him. He couldn't love her, and that hurt.

She pulled away from the warmth of his arms. She needed to protect her heart. Ryan offered physical safety. She needed to be grateful for that.

Faith pulled herself together with a big, deep breath.

"Thank you, and I'm sorry, Ryan. No one was supposed to see me like this. I'm fine now. I just need a minute to wash my face. Then I'll be down for dinner."

"Faith, it's okay to be upset. You've been through a terrible experience. I know you must be scared and hurt. Maggie and I will do what we can to help. I want you to know that I'm here for you. Whatever you need."

"Thank you," she wanted to tell him she needed him. She needed him to love her the way she loved him.

But that was foolish. He never could love someone as damaged as she was. She was too broken. A man like Ryan wanted someone strong. She felt so weak and helpless. She needed to distance herself from him.

"I'll see you in a minute." Ryan wiped a tear from her cheek, "I'm starving, so don't make me wait too long," he joked.

Then she was alone again. She splashed water on her face and wiped it with the soft hand towel hanging beside the sink. She breathed in a deep, cleansing breath and started praying. She spilled the pain in her aching, vulnerable heart to the Lord. As she prayed, she felt a peace settle in her soul. She checked her face in the mirror; it was a little brighter. She then gathered herself, put on a smile, and went to dinner.

Ryan went down the stairs to Maggie's dining room. The table held a steaming pot of beef stew and a loaf of homemade bread.

"I'm glad I made stew. It stays hot. I hope Faith is comfortable here."

"No one could be uncomfortable in your house."

"I know she's been through something terrible."

"From what I heard tonight, she's been through much worse."

"That poor, sweet girl."

"She's strong. She's resilient. She'll bounce back."

Then she walked into the room.

"Ryan said there was dinner ready? I just realized that I'm starving."

"Well, I hope you like beef stew."

"Sounds great and smells delicious."

They sat down and ate. After dinner, they pulled out a deck of cards and played rummy. Soon, Ryan could see that Faith was fading fast. Her eyes looked tired, and she was starting to head bob.

"I think it's time you went to bed, Faith. You're barely awake now."

"Honey, you must be exhausted. Why don't you go lie down?"

"I don't know if I'll be able to sleep."

"You're falling asleep right now. You'll rest better in bed."

"I need to be vigilant. What if he…."

"Trust me. I will keep you safe. No one is getting in this house tonight."

"Okay. I trust you, Ryan. I'll say goodnight right now. What time do you need me to get up, Maggie? I don't want to mess up your morning routine."

"I'm an early riser. I'll be up and ready by five."

"Okay, I'll try and be up by five."

"Sleep in a little. Maybe you should call in and take a day off tomorrow. Dr. A would understand."

"No. I'll be ready in the morning. I don't want anyone else to know what happened."

"I wonder what Ashley will think or say? Didn't she think that psycho was her boyfriend.?" Ryan wondered.

"He was leading her on. He said it was to get to me. I'm sure she'll be furious with me. She already doesn't like me."

"She's just jealous of your…."

Ryan shot Maggie a quick look.

"… of your… friendship with Ryan."

"Now she'll hate me; she's told me before that Charles, aka Charlie, was in love with her. She'll never believe that I didn't do something to steal him away from her."

"Don't worry about Ashley. She's not going to hurt you; Maggie and I won't let her. It's not your fault that she started dating that psycho."

"I feel bad for her; I didn't know he was a psycho at first. He can be very smooth and convincing. I didn't realize what he was till it was too late. It's my fault he's even here at all. If I hadn't gotten involved with him… no one would get hurt."

"Faith! Don't talk like that. You didn't know he would turn out this way. He manipulated you. Lots of girls have fallen for the wrong guy and gotten hurt. I'm so sorry that it happened to you. But don't blame yourself." Ryan was vehement as he put a comforting arm around her shoulders.

"Easier said than done. If I had just had patience and listened to my conscience…."

"Everyone makes mistakes in judgment sometimes," he tilted her face to look into his eyes, "Everyone."

"I guess I know. I just can't help my feelings."

"Feelings can lie," Ryan said.

"How can you know what's true?"

"Listen to the promises of God," Maggie told her, "He loves you; He has your best interest at heart."

"I know; I just have a hard time trusting sometimes."

"Rest on His promises. I think you ought to try to go and get some sleep. You've been through a lot!"

"Don't worry; I'll be here. You're safe." Ryan vowed.

"You are right; it's time I went to bed."

"Goodnight, Honey. Sleep will do you good." Maggie engulfed her in a hug.

"Rest, I'll be here," Ryan reassured her, taking both hands in his.

"Thank you, and goodnight," Faith reluctantly pulled away.

He wanted to pull her into his arms and kiss her, but tonight was not the time. What she needed was a guardian, not a boyfriend, not tonight. He would have to wait for the right time to tell her everything in his heart.

After she went to bed, Maggie sat beside him on her over-stuffed blue couch.

"Ryan, are you ready for me to say I told you so?"

"What do you mean?"

"You're in love with Faith."

"Is it that obvious?"

"I tried to warn you; love creeps up on you slowly."

"It hit me like a flash tonight."

"You may have realized it in a flash, but this has been happening a minute at a time."

"But I wasn't in love with her until I saw her through the window in that psycho's arms until I thought I could lose her."

"I've watched you, day by day, from that first week you were smitten, and I've seen you fall deeper in love as each day passes."

"I've only really kissed her twice."

"Love isn't just a physical thing, though that is part of it. You've chosen her every day you've sought her out. I know how hard you've worked to spend time with her. On top of that, you're trying to be a better man. I heard about your apology to Ashley."

"That was God. I've started listening. It was God who got me to Faith's apartment in time. I could feel Him pressing me on; I didn't even hit one red light."

"If you listen to God, he won't steer you wrong about whom to love. I believe you and Faith are right for each other."

"I just hope Faith sees things the way you do."

"Oh, I'm sure she does."

"Maggie, I think I screwed it up."

"How?"

"When I started trying to date her, I told her I wasn't looking for a permanent relationship. I'm afraid she won't think I'm serious about her."

"Then tell her."

"I want to do it when the time is right. I don't want to do anything that might hurt my chances. Charles did a number on her; I don't know if she can trust me."

"She trusts you now."

"Only as a protector. I want more."

"Be patient with her. I'm sure she loves you. You two need to talk things out."

"I'll try."

"In matters of the heart, there is no trying- only doing. Hurry up, too. Don't make that poor girl wait any longer for you."

"I'll know when the time is right."

Maggie gave him one of her motherly hugs and bid him goodnight.

"You can stay in Doyle's old room."

"I'm sitting up tonight. I said I'd keep you both safe, and I will."

"Don't stay up all night. Try and sleep a little. I've got my home alarm on. Doyle has guys patrolling the area. You need to be sharp for school tomorrow."

"I'm not sure I could sleep, even if I wanted to."

Maggie went to bed, but Ryan sat up till early in the morning; not only was he watching, but he was also praying. He needed help and guidance to win Faith and keep her safe.

Chapter 19

Faith had slept poorly. Every time she fell asleep, she relived those terrible moments with Charles, not just being found, but the years she'd spent with him before she escaped. Finally, she found her bag. She took her tablet from her overnight bag and found the Bible app. She found herself rereading Psalm 91. She prayed again for her safety and Ryan's and Maggie's. A sense of peace soothed her heart, and she could drift back to sleep for a couple of hours. The sound of her alarm woke her, and she wished she could curl up and go back to bed. But she needed to get up; she had to face what promised to be a trying day. She reminded herself that God would give her the strength to face the day ahead. She got dressed quickly and went downstairs.

She saw the last thing she'd expected. Ryan was in one of Maggie's big pink aprons, dusted with flour. He was singing as he made pancakes. She could smell bacon and eggs as well. Faith couldn't help but smile as she watched him. He caught her eye and sang into the spatula. That cracked her up, and she started laughing.

"I see you're up, and you look ravenous. Come have some of my famous flapjacks."

"I didn't know you cooked. Where's Maggie?"

"She's already had hers and is finishing up getting ready."

"Oh, am I slowing you down?"

"I've been up for hours. I'm going to take you to work today."

"Well, I'll hurry."

"Sit down and eat."

"Okay, it smells delicious."

"It should. I'm using my mom's secret recipe."

He brought her a plate overflowing with pancakes, bacon, and eggs. He sat next to her at Maggie's kitchen table.

"I can't eat all of this!"

"Of course, you can't with that attitude," he laughed.

She took a big bite and sighed, "This is delicious!"

"Glad you like it."

"What is in these pancakes? Chocolate chips and vanilla?"

"Can't tell. It's a secret recipe."

"Well, they are to die for. I usually just have coffee and toast. This is luxury."

"As long as we're staying with Maggie, get used to it."

She felt her heart sink. She couldn't stay here indefinitely and would soon have to go home. What if they couldn't find Charles? She'd have to break her lease and move. It would be Dallas all over again.

"I can't stay here indefinitely. I need to go back to my apartment. I don't want to keep putting Maggie in danger. Besides, she doesn't want me to live with her. She has a family and a life."

"You can't return to your apartment until we find Charles."

"You don't know how long it will take to find him or even if you will find him. He's brilliant and dangerous. He never gives up! I'll never be free of him."

"Hey, Faith, I'll keep you safe. I'm not going to rest till we've got him locked away. Now try and cheer up and eat your breakfast."

"I'll try. It is good."

"When you're ready, let me know, and we'll get to work."

"Thank you, Ryan, for everything."

Then he left her alone with her breakfast and her thoughts. Her dismal thoughts made it hard to finish eating; the food kept getting stuck in her throat. She managed a few more bites and decided it was time to go to school. She didn't want to make Ryan late. Maggie came in as she finished and put her dishes in the sink.

"Faith, Honey, I'm headed out. Ryan wants to take you to work."

"I can go with you."

"Ryan won't be easy in his mind if he's not got his eye on you."

"That's why I feel so safe with him."

"You're good for him, and I think he's good for you too."

"He's a good man."

"You should give him a chance."

"I don't think he wants one."

"I thought you two were dating."

"Whatever we're doing, he made it clear he doesn't want anything permanent."

"I won't stick my nose in your business. I think the two of you are good for each other."

"I know he's a good man. I know he makes me feel safe. I don't want to get my hopes up. He doesn't need someone with all my baggage. Especially baggage like Charles."

"Ryan doesn't care about your past. Trust him."

Just then, Ryan sauntered in. He had an adoring smile for them both.

"What are you girls gossiping about?"

Faith felt her face heat up with embarrassment. She didn't want him to know that she was talking about their relationship, whatever it was.

"Don't worry about it, Honey. Just a little girl talk. Are you two coming?" Maggie covered for them.

"We'll be behind you."

"I'll see you two at school."

Then Maggie left for work.

Ryan smiled, and Faith couldn't help but smile back. He looked so handsome and strong in his uniform. It took her breath away when he winked at her and asked, "Are you ready?"

"I just have to get my school things and my coat."

"I see you're wearing that red dress," she felt her cheeks flush with pleasure, "I like it."

"Thank you."

"Can I get your things for you?"

"You don't have to do that."

"It's my pleasure."

"Well, I don't know where you put it last night when we arrived."

"It's in the living room, by the table. I got it," he went and picked up her heavy school bag, "Your purse is over here too."

"I'll get it."

He took her coat and held it for her to put on. As she put it on, he wrapped her in his arms. He held her a moment longer than necessary. She could feel her heartbeat speed up, and he looked into her eyes. For a moment, she thought he was going to kiss her.

"Faith... I..."

She thought he was going to say something else.

"Yes?"

"I want you to feel safe today. Don't worry. Doyle's going to have some cruisers driving by the school. This school is mine. I'll keep it safe," he let her go.

"I don't want to face Ashley. I'm sure she hates me now. Do you think Ashley knows?"

"I don't know. Don't worry. Maggie and I will keep her away from you. You ready?"

"Ready as I'll ever be," she looped her purse over her shoulder, "Let's go."

Ryan led her out the door and locked up. He walked her to his truck and opened the door for her. She climbed in, and he shut the door. Then he got in, and they drove off to the school.

Faith was restrained and quiet on the ride to the school. She was strangely awkward. There were things in her heart she longed to say. She couldn't let him know what she felt. He had been crystal clear that he wanted to keep things casual. She had agreed, not realizing that he was so amazing. She thought the walls around her heart had been insurmountable, but Ryan had sneaked in and circumvented her defenses. Now, she regretted agreeing to their non-commitment relationship. Ryan was the man of her dreams. He was a good man, a Christian man, a strong man. He was all of the things she admired. She quickly prayed to surrender her feelings for Ryan to God. She felt better.

"Ryan, what should I do about Ashely?"

"I don't know. I'm definitely the last person to ask for advice about Ashley. I know I didn't handle her well. Even my apology went south. She hates me more than she could ever hate you. I admit I mistreated her. I'm ashamed of my actions. I don't want to make that mistake again."

"I understand," she knew he was telling her he wasn't interested in anything serious with her. That hurt. He'd warned her not to get attached. It was her fault for letting herself fall for him.

She felt the tears coming and blinked them back, but her sniffle was louder than expected.

"Faith? Are you okay?"

"I'm fine," she said. She didn't want him to know she was crying about him.

"Don't worry about today. Don't be anxious- it's something I'm learning about the Lord. He doesn't want us to be full of anxiety."

"I know. Things crowd around me sometimes, and I feel like I can't get out."

"Trust in God, and trust in me. I'll keep you safe."

She thought he could keep her body safe, but he was dangerous to her heart.

They kept driving in silence to the school.

He was clenching and unclenching his hands, wishing they were around Ryan Madsen's throat. He was seething with anger. He'd held her in his arms and then lost her. That policeman: Ryan Madsen. He was a problem. The man was like Faith's shadow. To be so close only to lose her.

Now, he had to go back into hiding. He'd gone to Ashley's. It had been a bit tricky. He'd gotten there before the police could contact her. Fortunately, Ashley was entirely under his control.

He told her that Faith had lied to the police. He told her that Faith was jealous of his relationship with her. He told her that Faith was unhappy with Ryan. Ryan had been cruel to her, unfaithful to her. He said that he had run into Faith after school, and she had invited him to her home, and he had gone there innocently. That she had come on to him. Then Ryan showed up and lost his head. Faith had lied to him, and in a rage, Ryan had called the police, and he and Faith had made up lies about him. To hurt him, her, and their relationship.

Ashley had believed him, of course. The police hadn't come looking for him at Ashley's. He'd briefed her on what to tell the cops if they tried to talk to her. He'd told her what to tell the other teachers if Faith or Ryan tried to spread their story about him. Ashley could turn the other teachers against Faith and the policeman. If he could separate Faith from the others, she would again be his for the taking.

He decided he would visit the house Faith had stayed in the previous night. He had seen her there before, always with Ryan. The old lady's house would be a perfect target. He would send a clear message. Faith was off-limits. He would make sure that the old lady stayed clear of Faith. He would destroy all her relationships. The only person she would have left would be him. Then they would be back to the way they were before, and they would be happy.

When he had her back, he would be able to breathe again. Faith was as essential as air to him. He knew she felt the same way, too. He had been watching her so closely. He had seen her *panic attacks. She needed him. He didn't understand why she let herself suffer without him. She had wanted to go with him last night. She missed him. She needed him as much as he needed her. It was Ryan who would pay.*

Chapter 20

"Faith! Are you okay?" Evon's concerned face alerted her that word of last night had gotten out.

"I'm fine," she told her as they walked down the hallways together to pick up their class at the gym.

"I heard you had a visitor last night."

"Why did Maggie tell you?"

"It wasn't Maggie. Ashley says the police are hunting her boyfriend Charlie because of you. She's saying horrible things about you and Ryan."

"Her *boyfriend* is Charles, my ex-fiancé. He found me. He came to my apartment and tried to take me with him by force. If Ryan hadn't shown up and called the police, he would have succeeded. I had to stay at Maggie's last night. Ryan sat up most of the night, watching for Charles."

"Oh, Faith! Thank God for Ryan."

"Do you think the others believe her?"

"I don't know. I'm sure Maggie will set the record straight. So will Ryan."

"Evon, what if they believe her? This will be just like my school in Dallas. I'll have to find a new job."

"Faith, the truth will out."

"But this could hurt Ryan."

"He's a big boy. He can handle anything Ashley dishes out. She's had it out for him for a while."

"He doesn't deserve that."

"You don't either."

"Evon, what am I going to do?"

"Tell your side."

"I hate for it all to come out. They'll think differently of me."

"Do it for Ryan."

"I just want to hide."

"You've got to be strong. Maggie and Ryan will have your back. I've got your back. Ryan won't let Ashley hurt you."

"I hate being so dependent on him."

"He doesn't mind."

"I can't let myself depend on him. He's not in it for the long haul. He told me he doesn't do serious. I should have listened to you. I've fallen for him, and he doesn't want me."

"Don't be so sure of that."

Then, the talk stopped as they gathered their class and headed to start their day.

Ryan was gritting his teeth and trying not to curse. He was boiling mad. Ashley was spreading lies about Faith and him. She was trying to destroy them. But it gave him an idea of where to look for Charles. Ashley must have heard these lies from him. She must have known where he was. He might even be staying with her. He would call Doyle and tell him. He should talk to Ashley first. He didn't have long to wait.

The tall woman came down, tossing her long dark hair over her shoulders. With her hairstyle and her eyes, she could easily be Faith's sister. He realized that the madman was trying to make Ashley into Faith. That was so sick. Charles must be sick and insane. Who knew what lies the man had filled Ashley with?

"Ryan! Why are you persecuting Charlie? I knew you were plotting to ruin my relationship."

"Ashley, Charlie is lying to you."

"He wouldn't. He loves me."

"Charlie isn't who he says he is."

"You're just jealous."

"I've talked to him. He told me his real name. His real desire. Don't believe him. He doesn't love you."

"He loves me."

"He's a psycho."

"Charlie is the most wonderful man. He told me all about Faith and you."

"His real name is Charles Meredith. He dated Faith, and he hurt her. He tried to abduct her last night. He will hurt you, too."

"Charlie would never hurt me. He told me that Faith was trying to steal him from me."

"Faith would never do that."

"You've driven her to it. You're treating her like you treated me."

"I've apologized to you. I'm sorry I hurt you. But Faith is innocent in all of this."

"She's jealous."

"Ashley, I don't want you to get hurt. If you know where he is, please let the police know."

"I would never betray Charlie."

"Don't you see what he's doing to you? He's making you into Faith."

"What do you mean? You're crazy. He loves me, loved me at first sight."

"Then why have you changed your eyes? Why have you changed your hair? Why have you changed your style?"

"I don't know what you're talking about. You're just being insulting."

"You changed contacts- to Faith's eye color. You've changed your hair- to Faith's hair color."

"*My* eyes, *my* hair- I am nothing like Faith! I am my own person. Charlie loves *me*."

"Ashley. He's deceiving you."

"You're just jealous."

"Please, for your own sake, talk to the police."

"I've got to go; my planning time is nearly over. You need to leave Charlie alone. I won't help you hurt the man I love. The man who loves *me*."

"Ashely!" he called after her as she stormed down the hall toward her classroom.

As soon as Ashley had stormed off, Ryan hurried to the office.

"Mrs. Brown? I need to make a call. Can I step into the supply closet?"

"I'll get the key."

He stepped into the supply closet for privacy, as he called Doyle.

"Doyle, I've got a lead on Charles."

"Tell me;" he was all business.

"Ashely Sheridan has been dating Charles Meredith. He's been using the alias Charlie Meridian. She came to the school today spreading lies about what happened last night. She could only have known that Charles was with Faith the previous night from him. Maggie and I kept quiet about it because Faith asked us to. I think that he might be staying with Ashley."

"I'll look into it, but I can't get in without a warrant."

"Ashley won't cooperate. That man has her under his thumb."

"I'm not sure there's much I can do if she's protecting him."

"Attempted kidnapping is a crime."

"I'll look into it."

"Thank you."

"How is she today?" Doyle switched gears.

"I know she's having a hard time with Ashley spreading lies about her."

"Poor thing, she doesn't deserve that. She's strong, and she can handle it."

"But she shouldn't have to. I'm doing my best to set the record straight."

"You care about her, don't you?"

"More than I should."

"Why not go for it?"

"She doesn't need that in her life right now. What she needs is a protector. I can wait till she's ready."

"Have you asked her what she needs?"

"What if she doesn't need me?"

"But what if she does? Talk to her. You're a brave guy; don't let her get away."

"I've got to get back to my post. Try looking at Ashley's."

"You got it, brother."

Ryan thought about Doyle's words. He was afraid that Faith didn't need him. He realized how much he needed her. Last night, he'd known that he loved her for keeps. Now, he just needed to keep her safe. There would be time to talk about love when the threat was gone.

He gave himself a moment to imagine what life with Faith would be like. He could picture it all in his mind. Her smile greeted him across the table. Her raucous laugh rang in his ears. He was kissing her sweet lips. Life could be so good. He shook himself from his pleasant reverie. He needed to focus on the job at hand.

As he was pacing back and forth at his post, Maggie came running up to him with a look of fear in her eyes.

"Ryan, I just got a call from the alarm company. The alarm at my house went off."

"Did anyone get in?"

"The cameras show the door busted in, and the motion detectors inside the house went off. The alarm company called the police. I'm waiting to hear more."

"Maggie!"

"Do you think it was Charles?"

"That seems likely."

"Ryan. Does that mean he knows that Faith was there last night?"

"Probably. How did he know?"

"If he knows, she's not safe at my house."

"I knew she should have stayed at my place last night."

"I thought my home would be safe…."

"Both of you will stay at my house tonight. It's the only way to keep both of you safe. Are you going home now?"

"I need to get there soon."

"Is Doyle meeting you there?"

"Yes."

"Be safe. Don't go in until Doyle or another officer is with you. Faith said Charles would hide and wait for her."

"I will."

Ryan knew he had to tell Faith. She would be so upset.; she would blame herself. There was nothing for it. He must tell her. She needed to know.

He had Mrs. Brown call Faith to the office so that he could talk to her. He was pacing. He didn't want to see the hurt that would be in her eyes. He also knew he'd have difficulty convincing her to stay with him. He wouldn't be easy if he couldn't keep both eyes on Faith. As he paced across the floor, he saw her coming to him; her eyes were full of worry.

"Ryan, what's happened? Have they found him?"

"Not yet, but Maggie's house was broken into this morning."

"Oh no!"

"We don't know that it was Charles."

"Ryan, I'm not a fool. It isn't just a coincidence. He knew where I was staying. Now Maggie is in danger. Where is she going to stay? Her home isn't safe- because of me."

"Stop it, Faith!"

"Ryan, you know Charles is only here, terrorizing my friends because of me."

"It's not your fault!"

"I'm going back to my apartment tonight. I won't put anyone else in danger."

"No, you're not! You're staying with me."

"I will not."

"Then I'm staying with you. I won't let you be alone. I'll get someone to stay with us. Maybe Maggie again, or Ellie, even Evon."

"I won't put anyone else in danger."

"Maggie could stay with us; I'd feel better about her if she stayed elsewhere."

"But Ryan, it's not safe."

"I can take care of myself and you."

"I don't know, Ryan."

"Faith, I need you to do this for me."

"Why, Ryan?"

He wasn't sure he should tell her yet. He wasn't sure she'd welcome it.

"I… care about you."

"I care about you too, and Maggie; I can't let you put yourselves in danger."

"I can take care of both of you. Faith, I'm a cop. A good one. It's my job to take care of people. I want to take care of you."

"Okay. I will."

"I'll try to get someone to stay with us."

"Thank you."

"We'll stop by Maggie's and get your stuff. We can stop at your place, too."

"Okay." Her head drooped with defeat.

"Chin up! God is strong, and so are you. Don't be anxious about anything. Remember? You are under His wing and mine. I'll see you after school."

"I've got some things I have to get done after school."

"I'll wait. Can I help?"

"I don't know. How are you at cutting out lamination?"

"I used to help my mom with that; I'm the fastest scissors in town."

That garnered a smile.

"Then come by when you're done with your rounds."

"I'll be there. By the way, I still like that dress."

"Thanks," she blushed as she walked back to her room.

Chapter 21

Faith was nervous as she rode to Maggie's house with Ryan to get her things. She wasn't sure what they would find waiting for them there. She was praying that the damage would be minimal. Unfortunately, she knew Charles; he would be as destructive as possible. He had wrecked multiple motel rooms while hunting her after their breakup. She would do her best to undo the damage, but inevitably, she would be left with a massive bill for damages. She hated Maggie suffering for her kindness to her.

"Ryan, did Maggie say how bad it was?"

"She didn't tell me."

"I feel awful."

"It will be all right," he reassured her.

When they arrived, the place was nearly empty. When they went inside, Maggie was sitting on what was left of her couch. The room was a disaster. Throw pillows slashed open and thrown around the room. There was a trail of destruction up the stairs and in all the bedrooms. Drawers were pulled out, and some were thrown on the ground. Belongings were scattered and littering the floor.

In the room Faith had slept in the night before, her bag was ripped open, and her things were strewn across the bed.

"Oh, Maggie!" she cried, "Maggie, I'm so sorry! Did he take anything?"

"Not of mine that I can tell. I've been looking for it all day. All my jewelry, money, and important documents are still here. The cash I keep around the house is all still here. Mostly, there is just property damage."

"I-I'm sorry. You have been so good to me; this is how you're repaid. I don't know how to make it up to you."

"Honey, it's all just things. Things can be replaced and repaired. I'm so thankful we were all at school today."

"Faith, look through your things, see if anything is missing."

"Okay, I didn't bring much with me, and most of that is my school stuff."

She carefully combed through the wreckage of the room. She was picking her clothes off the floor.

"My pajamas are missing!"

"Do you think he took them?"

"I think so. He used to take things when he would break into wherever I was staying. He would also leave things for me."

"Have you found anything that doesn't belong?"

"Let me look."

She started examining the area closely as if seeing a puzzle. Then, she lifted a silver charm bracelet from the bedside table.

"This is a bracelet he gave me when we first started dating. I sold it to a pawn shop when I left him."

She held it gingerly in her hand, the cold metal charms hanging against her fingers. She looked at it carefully. Her heart was beating rapidly like a hummingbird's.

"This charm. It's new. It's engraved. It says, 'Forever, my Love.' It's a message. He's not going to leave me alone. He'll never stop looking for me," cold settled in her bones.

"Faith, Look at me." Ryan crooned, "I've got your back. I'm here, and I'm not leaving you."

"Ryan, I'm not safe. I'll never be safe."

"Tonight, you're staying with me. Maggie is staying at Doyle's."

"Okay. Thank you. I don't want to bring you trouble, Ryan."

"I can take it. It's what I do."

She felt such a swell of love for him in her heart. If only he felt the same way. Ryan was everything she could want in a man. He was strong, masculine, courageous, handsome, and, most importantly, a Christian. None of the warnings her heart had given her about Charles were there. Except, he had told her he didn't want a serious relationship. And now she was in love with him. She had to rely on him for her safety. Being with him at home would make it even harder for her. She had to find a new solution. She was breaking her heart.

Faith gathered what was left of her belongings, and they returned to her apartment. Ryan was on full alert.

"Faith, I'll go in first; you follow me. You'll probably need a few days of clothes to be on the safe side."

"I thought it would just be for tonight. Surely, there is somewhere I can go. Maybe a women's shelter? You don't want me to stay with you indefinitely. I won't do it," she looked out the window despondently.

"I need to know you're safe."

"I can find someplace else to stay that's safe."

"Surely, they'll find him soon. I have a feeling that they'll strike gold at Ashley's. Also, Maggie's security camera got a great shot of him."

"Maybe that will make Ashley stop spreading lies."

"I'm sorry she's lying about you. It's just because she hates me. I deserve it- you don't!"

"She hates me too. And I know that Charles is lying to her."

"Why would she listen to him? He's manipulating her."

"I was under his spell for a long time. He can be very…persuasive. He can be charming, and his lies sound like the truth. He is a narcissist and a master manipulator. I believed he loved me. He doesn't know what love is. Not the kind of love God gives. I didn't see or understand it for a long time, so I paid the price."

"I tried to tell her; she just got angrier at me."

"It's hard to hear that someone you love lies to you. That they are using you. That they don't love you."

"Someone needs to set her straight."

"I don't think she would listen to either one of us. You don't love her as she wants you to, and she believes I'm trying to steal her boyfriend. I don't know whom she'll listen to. But I worried about her. Charles is an abuser. He only cares about himself and what he wants."

"I can't fix it."

"Only God can."

Then he exited the truck, opened her door, and helped her out. They cautiously made their way to her apartment. Ryan was vigilant as they crossed the parking lot and climbed the stairs to her front door. She handed him her key, and he unlocked all the locks. He slowly opened the door.

"Faith, get behind me. I'll go first." He was all business. His hand was poised over the gun in its holster.

He started a slow sweep of the apartment, room by room. He called out, "Faith, it's all clear."

She breathed a deep breath she didn't realize she had been holding. She stepped further into her living room.

"Let's be quick."

"I don't know how much to pack."

"Enough for a week."

"A week!"

"Just until we find him."

"A week is too long."

"I can get someone to stay with us if that would make you more comfortable."

"Thank you, that's sweet of you."

"I'll call Evon."

"Okay, but that's not my main problem. I can't stay with you that long. You have a life. I have things I have to do. I can't let you put your life on hold for me."

"I don't have much of a life outside of work. You won't be putting me out. Besides, I like spending time with you."

Staying with Ryan would complicate things when he inevitably broke up with her. But where else was she supposed to go?

"Okay, one week. Then I'm going to find something else."

"You don't want to stay with me?" He was making his puppy dog eyes again.

"I don't want to be ungrateful. I do enjoy spending time with you, too. But I know fish and house guests start stinking after three days."

"That won't be a problem. Anyway, we should have Charles in custody by then."

"I hope so."

She began to pack her bag. Did she remember everything? She got a week's worth of clothes and underthings. She packed extra pajamas. Charles had taken her favorite pair when he tore up Maggie's place. Then she went to her jewelry box. She wanted the necklace her mother gave her for her birthday. She had forgotten it in her hurry last night. The necklace was gone. In its place hung her old engagement ring on a thick golden chain. She blanched. Her heart dropped. Had he done this before he left, or had he come back? Either way, she was scared. Faith knew that it was a message. He would never let her go.

"Faith? Are you ready?" called Ryan from the other room.

"I'm nearly done," she forced a cheerful note into her voice.

"What's wrong?" As she entered the room, Ryan asked, "You're as white as a sheet. Did you find something?"

"My cross necklace was gone," she had to tell him, "In its place was my old engagement ring on a chain."

"We know he was here last night. I doubt he came back today. He's not here now. You're safe."

"I know. I never did like that ring."

"Why? What kind of rings do you like?"

"It was too flashy. I like something more subtle. If a ring is too big, I tend to catch it on everything."

"Good to know."

"A ring's value is in who and where it came from. It was just a symbol of ownership to him."

"Not all men are like him, Faith. I'm not."

"I know," she did. Ryan was her ideal man.

His big cheesy smile appeared, and her heart flipped over.

"So, are you all packed and ready? I gave Evon directions to my place, and she'll meet us there."

"Thank you. You think of everything. I need to grab some shoes and my chargers."

When she was completely packed, Ryan opened her front door.

"Stay here. I'll come and get you once I know it's all clear."

Then she watched him walk to his truck and do a perimeter check around it. He came back up to her door and grabbed her bags from her.

"Lock up and follow me."

She did, and they got into the truck and drove to his home.

He pinched his nose at the bridge, staving off a headache. His head was throbbing. He needed a new plan. He had to find a way to take Faith away with him. If he could get her away with him, he would take her somewhere they could be alone together. He had a place already set up for them to be together. The two of them didn't need anyone or anything else. She had been happy with him and could be happy with him again. Together forever.

He swallowed two ibuprofens. The policeman had her. That man was a thorn in his side. He was everywhere. He was Faith's constant shadow. There had to be someplace where she was vulnerable. Somewhere, he could have leverage over her. She needed a little push, and she would return to him.

He had tried tearing up the old lady's house as a message. Come back, or someone will get hurt. That had the reverse effect. Now Faith was even tighter in Ryan's grasp.

An idea slowly started to take shape in his mind. There was a way to take her back and discredit the policeman. It would be tricky and dangerous. He would need Ashley's help.

He wasn't worried about Ashley's cooperation. She was his to control. It could damage her reputation, maybe even affect her job, but that didn't bother him. After all, she was only a tool.

It was risky. There was still an infinitesimal chance that Faith wouldn't come with him willingly. If he couldn't be with her, Ryan Madsen wouldn't either.

With his plan settled in his mind, he started to prepare.

Chapter 22

Ryan drove up to a brick house. It was a cozy split-level house with two bay windows like eyes looking out to the road. It had a chimney that spoke of cozy fires on cold nights. The front door had been painted red, and the look was charming. It didn't look like a house you'd expect a bachelor to live in.

When Ryan opened the door, they entered the living room. In front of the forty-inch smart TV was a large red and dark blue plaid sofa. Near the couch, there was a huge brown leather recliner. A coffee table sat between the sofa and the TV. Another oversized brown leather recliner was on the other side of the sofa.

While Ryan checked the house, Faith looked around the living room and hallway. Faith noticed the walls were covered with old family pictures; they seemed stuck in the recent past. There were pictures of a woman with brown curly hair and eyes the same baby blue as Ryan's. That must be his mother. She saw a picture of Ryan and Doyle in uniform, giving a thumbs-up sign. There was a picture of Maggie and the woman together smiling. It was like glimpsing into Ryan's past. She almost felt like she was snooping.

"It's all clear."

"Thank you for bringing me here and letting me stay. You are going way beyond the call of duty."

"Believe me; it's a pleasure."

"Ryan, why are you being so good to me?"

"I'm not doing anything special. Besides, I like spending time with you."

"I like spending time with you too. I'm just afraid you'll get tired of having me around. Soon. Charles always told me he was the only one who could put up with me."

"There's nothing to put up with. I like hanging out with you. You're funny, kind, and sweet. And when it comes down to it, nobody is always good company. I know I'm not."

"Thank you, you're pretty great yourself. I have more fun with you than anyone else." She couldn't believe she'd said that; she didn't want to be pushy. If he were going to commit to her, she'd have to move slowly and be patient. She also didn't need to get her hopes up. She came with a lot of baggage.

"Now, we agreed that we're going to have fun. Let me take your things."

"Ryan, I don't want to put you out. I can stay on the couch."

"Nonsense. I've got extra bedrooms. There's the master suite, so you'll have your own bathroom. All the privacy you want."

"Isn't that your bedroom?"

"No, it was Mom's. I've never had the heart to sleep in there. My room's been mine for as long as I can remember."

"I can't disturb your mom's room."

"Nonsense, it's not a shrine."

"In fact, let me go put some clean sheets on the bed."

"That's not necessary."

"I insist. Mom would have had a fit if she thought I didn't."

"Well, let me help at least. I insist."

"Okay, let me get your bags."

He carried her bags down the hallway into the room on the right. It was a spacious room with a king-size bed. There was an antique dresser set and an oversized vanity with a large mirror.

There were more pictures of Ryan, most of them of him as a child or teenager.

The bathroom was through a door on the left. It held a double sink and a long full bath. The toilet was in a little nook next to the sinks. It was a charming shade of blue, and funny cartoon fish were swimming on the walls.

"Ryan! This bathroom is adorable!"

"Thanks, I can't take credit for it; Mom decorated it." He said as he came in, bringing a set of sheets. She joined him, and they started changing the sheets and remaking the bed.

"We would have gotten along; she has great taste."

"I know you would have gotten along. Mom would have loved you."

"Thank you, again, for letting me stay. Hopefully, I won't impose for too long."

"It's not an imposition. I like having you around."

She felt a warmth spread when he said that. It felt nice to have Ryan want to spend time with her. It gave her a glimmer of hope. The bed was made quickly.

"When you get settled in, come into the kitchen. I'll make us a snack."

"Thank you. I'll be there in a moment."

She looked at the cozy room and pictured her spartan bedroom. She was so used to running that she feared for a place to feel like home. If she let herself feel too at home, it would be harder to leave when the inevitable happened, and she would have to pack up and go. If she didn't have to worry about Charles, she would love a chance to make somewhere feel like home. Her heart yearned to make a nest for herself. She longed for security and a place to belong. For a moment, she saw herself settled in this house with Ryan. That was the dream.

Ryan was pacing in the living room. He was excited. Faith was finally here. He could keep her safe. No more worrying about her, far from his help. He knew this house; it was his home base.

He had taken every precaution. Charles couldn't get in here. That thought settled him, and he stood by the fireplace, waiting for her to come in.

There was a ring at the doorbell. He tensed and looked at the video keypad. It was Evon's friendly face with a worried expression.

He opened the door and let her in.

"Ryan, is she okay?"

"She is now."

"Where shall I put my stuff?"

"Follow me." He led her to the spare bedroom down the hall.

As Evon put up her stuff, she said, "You made the right call having me stay over. She would be upset if Ashley heard you spent the night together."

"But I wouldn't do anything; you know that. Faith knows that too, doesn't she?"

"She trusts you."

"That's good."

"But you know Ashley would tell all kinds of lies about y'all if she thought y'all were alone."

"Ashley is a pain in my rear end."

"She's never gotten over you. She can't stand the thought that you and Faith are an item."

"We're not an item," he ruefully admitted.

"But you've got it bad for Faith. Anyone can see that."

"When you're ready, come into the living room, and we'll see what Faith wants to do." He said to change the subject.

"I get it. I'll be there in a minute."

He quickly returned to the living room to avoid a more awkward conversation. His newfound love was something that he wanted to treasure for himself. Maggie knew, but she was his other mother. He needed to tell Faith how he felt, but the timing seemed off. It had to be just right.

She walked into the room. He could see she was ready to relax. Her hair was flowing softly to her shoulders. Her face was clean and fresh, and the traces of tears on her cheeks were gone. She wore an oversized, black T-shirt that read, "Ten more minutes," and black pajama pants. She was beautiful.

"I hope you don't mind my PJs."

"You look adorable. I'm glad you're comfortable."

"Evon just got here. She's in the spare room at the end of the hall. What would you like to do? We can veg out on the couch and watch TV, or I have some games we could play."

"Vegging out and watching TV sounds heavenly."

"You have a seat. I will change out of uniform, and then I'll get us some snacks."

"Don't go to a lot of trouble over me."

Then he went upstairs to his room. He changed into a blue T-shirt and sweatpants then he went back to where she was waiting. Evon was there, too, in the recliner.

"Do you want a snack? I can pop some popcorn."

"That sounds great," Faith answered.

"I would love some popcorn."

"I can also make hot chocolate or coffee if you want."

"Hot chocolate. You're spoiling me." Faith's voice had a hint of pleasure.

"I agree. I never get waited on." Evon said.

"Faith, you've had a rough couple of days. You deserve a chance to relax." He went into the kitchen and started getting the snacks ready. "Just wait till you taste my hot chocolate; it's my secret recipe."

"Yummy. I can smell… cinnamon?"

"Just wait till you taste it."

He soon brought them a bowl of popcorn, returned to the kitchen, and got the big mugs of steaming hot chocolate.

"What do you want to watch?" he asked.

"I don't care." Faith was still standing by the fireplace, looking at the photos on the mantlepiece.

"Don't just stand there. Come, sit on the sofa next to me."

Faith sat down next to him on the sofa. Ryan scooted closer to her and wrapped his arm around her shoulder.

"How about I find us a movie? What do you like?"

"Nothing scary! I've had my fill of monsters."

"How about something funny?" Evon suggested.

"That works."

He flipped to the movie service and found a funny old slapstick comedy.

"I love old movies. I hope you like them. This one is hilarious. It's about a ridiculous girl, a scientist, a dinosaur bone, and a leopard."

"Sounds good," and she nestled into his embrace, to his delight. He could smell the soft scent of her hair. Vanilla was becoming his favorite smell.

He turned the movie on and felt peaceful. This is what he wanted his life to be like. Faith and him spending time together, not doing anything in particular. He thought that she fit so perfectly there beside him.

The only thing that brought him back to reality was Evon's boisterous laugh.

As they watched the movie, Faith got quiet, and her head fell onto his shoulder. She was asleep.

"She's worn out," Evon stated quietly.

"She's been through a lot."

"Just be careful."

"I would never hurt her."

"If you're not serious, you need to let her down ASAP."

"I just want her to be safe and happy."

"Me too," Evon stood up and yawned, "Well, I'm going to bed. Goodnight."

"See you in the morning."

When Evon left, he softly shook Faith.

"Faith, you're asleep. You'll be more comfortable in bed."

“Yes, I should go to bed.”

“Do you want me to tuck you in?”

“I can tuck myself in.” she laughed sleepily.

“Then, goodnight, Faith, sleep tight. If you need anything, holler. I’ll be upstairs.”

“Thank you. I think I’ll be able to sleep tonight.”

Then he helped her stand off the sofa, engulfing her in a strong embrace.

“Goodnight,” he couldn’t help himself. He bent his head down and kissed her ever so softly.

“Goodnight, Ryan,” she whispered. Then she hurried to her bedroom and shut the door.

Chapter 23

Faith shook herself. What was that? Ryan had kissed her. It had been such a gentle kiss. It felt so right. She was getting her hopes up for nothing. He had just been caught up in the moment. A kiss didn't mean he wanted to get serious. He'd kissed her before, which hadn't meant anything to him. She needed to give it to God. Faith prayed, "Heavenly Father, I'm scared. I'm lonely. I know I'm putting my faith in Ryan. Now I've fallen in love with him and don't know what to do. Help me put my trust and hope in You. You guide me and show me if it's Your will for me to be with Ryan. I put all of myself in your mighty hands. Please guard, guide, and keep me safe under your wings. In Christ's name, I pray. Amen."

Her heart felt lighter. Her exhaustion overcame her, and she fell asleep.

Before her alarm went off, Faith woke up. She could hear Evon's big laugh and smell coffee and something spicy. She thought about going back to sleep for fifteen more minutes, but the delicious aroma made her hungry. She hopped out of bed.

Faith dressed quickly and deftly ran a brush through her hair. She was in a hurry to get to the kitchen.

When she entered the blue kitchen, she found Evon and Ryan laughing at the kitchen table.

"Good morning." She saw that Evon was in a bathrobe and Ryan was already in his uniform.

"You're both early risers!"

"I didn't sleep much," Ryan admitted.

"I couldn't stay in bed with the smell of these breakfast burritos filling the house," Evon said, wiping her mouth.

"They do smell wonderful. Can I have some?"

"Of course, let me get you a plate. One or two?"

"One to start, and can I have some coffee too?"

"I'll get it; you sit down."

"Thank you. I've never been so spoiled."

"Well, you eat up Faith. I've got to go get dressed."

"I'll see you when you're ready. I still have to finish getting ready. My hair's a mess." Faith replied.

"I think you look gorgeous." He said, bringing her a plate and a cup of coffee.

Ryan's compliment made her blush happily.

"Thanks. By the way, this is delicious. I would never have believed you were such a good chef."

"My mom taught me to cook. She always said a man should know how to take care of himself. I can even sew on my buttons and darn holes in socks."

"I'm impressed."

"That's the idea."

"You're trying to impress me?"

"Of course."

She didn't know how to respond. So, she bit into the burrito and chewed furiously.

"Faith, I need to talk to you." He sat down at the yellow table next to her.

The breakup was coming. She could hear it in his words. She knew it was inevitable, but she wasn't ready. She took a breath and steeled herself for the pain.

"Wha-what's up?"

"I want you to know…"

"What?"

At that moment, Ryan's phone rang.

"Hello?" he was suddenly all business, "Yes, sir. That's great news!"

He ended the call.

"Faith!" his voice was excited, "They've caught him!"

"Charles?"

"He's in custody."

"Then it's over?"

"It depends on if he makes bail."

"Do you think he will? He's a wealthy man."

"I don't know."

"Ryan, does that mean I can go home?"

"If you want to…" his voice was disappointed.

"Ryan, I can't thank you enough for letting me stay. But I need to be home. Now, I must get ready for school. I'm free, Ryan. Free."

"Just wait till we know if he makes bail."

"Okay, Ryan."

"I'm glad. I want you to be safe."

"Do I have to do anything about it?"

"No, attempted kidnapping is a crime."

"I don't want to see him again if possible."

"You might have to testify against him in court."

"I could do that," she sighed, "I wonder where they picked him up?"

"I don't know many details; Doyle just wanted to let us know they had him in custody."

"It seems too good to be true. Freedom feels strange. I can't really grasp that I'm safe now. Am I?"

"If he doesn't make bail, he'll stay there until he comes before a judge."

"What about Ashley and the lies she's been telling? Isn't it our word against hers?"

"When they get your statements from Dallas, it will be open and shut."

"I don't know that they did anything about it in Dallas. I never pressed charges; I just left. It will be my word against his. And he is wealthy and connected."

"It will all work out. Pray about it. I've got your back."

"I know you do. Thank you."

"This makes it easier to tell you…"

"Tell me what?" her stomach sank; he was going to say goodbye.

"Faith, I…" he was stopped by the ringing of Faith's phone; she scrambled in her pocket to get it before it stopped ringing.

"Hello?" she answered.

"How dare you?"

"Ashley?"

Ryan whispered, "Put it on speaker."

Faith did.

"How dare you! Charlie is a good man. Why are you persecuting him?"

"Ashley, he's not who you think he is."

"I know his real name isn't Meridian. He told me he lived under an alias because you were trying to ruin him. He was afraid you would try to destroy him."

"That's not true. He's manipulating you."

"He said you'd try and say something like that. He told me all about you and how you hounded him for months. He doesn't love you. He loves me. Deal with it and stop trying to ruin his life."

"Ashley, I don't love Charles. I'm afraid of him."

"How could you be afraid of such a gentle, caring man."

"He's a monster. You don't know everything he did to me while we were dating."

"He was afraid you would lie about him. You need to get it through your head that it's over between you. He's made his choice."

"I don't want him! He will only hurt you like he hurt me."

"You don't need to keep lying about Charlie. If anyone needs a warning, it's you. Ryan will play fast and loose with you. If anyone is untrustworthy, it's him."

"Leave Ryan out of this."

"He's in it too. He's out to get Charlie. He can't stand to see me happy."

"Ashley…" Ryan growled.

"Ryan? I should have known you'd be with Faith. You're probably both plotting against him. Just leave him alone!"

Then, there was silence on the other side of the line. Ashley had ended the call.

"Ryan, what am I going to do? No one will believe me."

"I believe you. Maggie does, too. We'll find evidence against him at her house. Surely, he left a fingerprint somewhere in that carnage."

"He's too smart to have done that."

"Maybe Maggie's camera will show his face."

"I'm not getting my hopes up."

"Don't despair. You're safe with me. I won't let him hurt you."

"He's smart, wealthy, and well-connected. He has powerful lawyers at his disposal. I'll never be truly free."

"Yes, you will. He will slip up. Then we'll catch him."

"I wish I was as sure as you are."

"Remember, God is protecting you, and so am I."

"I don't know what I'd do without you."

"I'm not going anywhere," he stood up and went around the table to where she sat, and he leaned down and placed a chaste kiss on her forehead, sealing the promise.

He sat quietly in the interrogation room, deliberately still and quiet. He had put on an expression of righteous indignation. He clenched his jaw till it hurt. He was waiting for his lawyers. He had his story; it would be her word against his, and he was well connected. Ashley would back him up. She would tell a tale of jealousy and lies. Faith was just obsessed with him. He had only come here to check on her well-being and had fallen for Ashley. Deceit came easily to him. He was a master manipulator.

Besides, it was for Faith's own good. He was sure she still wanted him; he had seen how unhappy she was. She was desperate for him to come and take her with him. Once he had her back under his control, she would be happy. He knew he could make her happy. She just needed a chance to come back to her senses.

He sat up as his lawyers arrived. He spun his tale of Faith's obsession and Officer Ryan's misunderstanding of the situation. He dismissed the idea of having a hand in the break-in at the old woman's house. He assured them he didn't even know the woman.

He had been masked and worn gloves when he tore through her place. He had hidden his souvenir; the pajamas Faith had worn. He could smell her scent on them. He had also been careful about fingerprints on the charm bracelet, ring, and necklace. He would never slip up so stupidly.

He claimed to have been at Ashley's all day. She would assume he was. She had been at school. When he was done, Faith sounded like just another crazed ex-girlfriend. He made the policeman seem like a man who had gotten too closely involved with a teacher at his school and had lost all objectivity. His lawyers had plenty of ammunition. They could even argue that Ryan was a bad cop who used his power to get women. Ashley would readily agree to anything that discredited him.

His lawyers hadn't failed him. He left the police station triumphantly. All charges had been dismissed. The police chief and DA apologized. He would have to be more careful in his pursuit of

*Faith. But now he knew nothing would stop him from having her
for his own.*

Chapter 24

Ryan stood up and threw up his hands in exasperation. Why was Faith so stubborn? She was being completely unreasonable. He gritted his teeth and stifled a growl. The clock in the teacher's lounge was ticking down the minutes. Their lunch break would be over soon, and she still hadn't agreed to his plan.

"Faith, for the last time, come home with me."

"I can't impose on you."

"It's not an imposition."

"I want to stand on my own."

"What if he made bail?"

"You told me this morning that he was in custody."

"Doyle hasn't heard anything yet about it."

"Then I should be able to go to my apartment."

"If he gets out, that's the first place he'll go."

"I can't stay with you indefinitely."

"Don't you trust me to keep my hands to myself?"

"I trust you. But people will talk. Ashely will talk."

Ryan thought for a moment and then had a stroke of genius. The perfect solution. He instantly changed his tone; he was in earnest.

"Then… marry me,"

"Are you crazy?"

"I'm as serious as I can be," his voice was gentle and rang with truth.

"No, you must be crazy. You told me you don't get serious with any woman."

"You're not any woman," he got down on one knee in the middle of the teacher's lounge, "I love you, Faith Rogers. Will you marry me?"

"You must be crazy! I won't let you sacrifice yourself on the marriage altar out of some false sense of chivalry."

"Faith, I love you," he held her gaze and let his eyes tell her how much he loved her.

"Really?"

"I have for a while, but I didn't realize it till Charles almost took you from me. I've fallen a little more in love with you every day since you walked through the front door."

"You are serious!"

"Let me prove it."

Then he stood up, pulled her into his arms, and kissed her gently. He let his lips do the talking and poured out his heart as he kissed her.

He ended the kiss and looked deep into her eyes.

"Believe me?" He kept her in the circle of his arms.

"Yes, and I love you too."

"Then what's stopping you? Marry me."

"I will," Faith said with tears in her eyes.

He sealed his promise with another kiss.

"Now that that is all taken care of… what were we talking about?" he grinned.

"I still won't stay at your place tonight," she stepped away from him.

"Then let's get married tonight."

"That is crazy! We can't get married that quickly. Don't you need some time to get used to the idea?"

"Honestly, no. I know that I want to be with you forever. Why can't we elope?"

"You're crazy. We wouldn't be able to get things done in time to elope tonight. We'd need a license; we'd need a preacher; we'd need witnesses. What about my parents? They would be upset if I got married without them present. It takes a little planning, even to elope. I'm not going to marry you tonight. That's crazy."

"Okay," he gave up. She'd agreed to marry him, and he could wait.

"At least give me a day or two to get things together!"

"I can do that. Why don't you stay somewhere else tonight? It worries me that you are staying in your apartment."

"I'll be fine. I won't open the door for anyone; I'll even change the locks. You can check every inch of the apartment."

"I have a compromise."

"What?"

"Let's get connecting rooms at a hotel. I can keep an eye on you."

"I can do that. I hate being so helpless."

"You agreed to marry me. We are partners now. I will take care of you, and you will take care of me."

"So far, I've only taken, and you've done all the giving."

"That's not true," he took her hands in his, "You've given me your love and trust. You've taught me how to love again. I was just drifting after Mom died. You showed me how to be a man again. You gave me a reason to be better than I was. I want to be worthy of you."

"When you put it that way, I guess I am pretty great," she laughed.

"I think so," he pulled her back into his arms.

Just then, Ashley rushed in like a whirlwind. She stopped abruptly and stared at them.

"Well, isn't this some inappropriate behavior? I'll be contacting Doctor Abernathy immediately," Ashley stormed out the door.

"Wait! It's not what you think." Ryan called.

"I don't know what else it could be."

"I just asked Faith to marry me, and she said yes."

"What?" Ashley looked incredulously at the two of them. "After throwing yourself at Charlie and getting him arrested, are you suddenly going to get engaged?"

"I never threw myself at Charles. He is unhinged. He's lying to you." Faith said.

"He warned me that you might try to hurt us like that."

"Ashley, listen to me. Charles is bad news. He's using you."

"You are a liar, Ryan. I can't believe this fool has agreed to marry you. She is nothing but a flirt. She won't be faithful to you."

"That isn't true. I don't want Charles. I left Texas to escape him."

"You are both liars. Charlie loves me. He is a wonderful man. I'm going to talk to Dr. A. right now. You two are going to be in a lot of trouble," and she stomped out of the room.

"Ashley!" Ryan tried to get her to come back, but she was already at the end of the hallway.

"Ryan, am I going to get into trouble?"

"It will be all right. When I explain things, he'll see the truth of what is going on."

"I can't get into trouble. I love this job."

"I won't let you get into trouble. Now go on and get to your class; it's nearly lunchtime. I'll see you after school. We're going to get you a ring."

"Thank you, Ryan," she said as she ran out of the teacher's lounge and down the hall to her classroom.

Ryan knew he needed to find Dr. Abernathy and explain things hopefully before Ashley got them into trouble. He purposefully strode out the door and to the main office.

Ashley was waiting impatiently at Dr. A's door and tapping her foot when he arrived.

"Mrs. Brown? I need to speak to Dr. Abernathy." Ryan said.

"You'll have to wait; he's in with a parent. Then it's Ms. Sheridan's turn."

"It will only take a moment, and I've got my rounds to do yet," he turned on the charm.

"All right, Officer Madsen. You can go in after he's done with the parent. I'll call you and let you know when he's free."

He was hesitant to leave with Ashley standing at Dr. Abernathy's door. Then, he had a stroke of genius; he would beat her to the punch.

"Before I go, Mrs. Brown, I'd like you to be one of the first to know. Faith Rogers and I just got engaged. I surprised her in the break room on her planning time."

He heard an angry "Harrumph!" from Ashley.

"How romantic!" Mrs. Brown gushed, "I'd heard you two were dating, but I didn't realize you were serious. Congratulations! Is that what you wanted to tell Dr. Abernathy?

"Yes, I just wanted to let him know before any rumors started flying around. I'm taking her to get a ring today after school. Now I've got to hurry to do my lunch rounds."

"Does Mrs. Foster know yet?"

"No one except Ms. Sheridan knows; she came in right after Miss Rogers said yes."

"Really, Ms. Sheridan? That's so romantic."

"Thank you for giving me the scoop! Is it a secret still, or can I share the good news?"

"Feel free to share. We're telling everyone. See you later; I've got rounds."

Chapter 25

He could just be happy now that he had stolen Ashley's ammunition. He hummed quietly as he went down the halls, checking each room and double-checking the outside doors. He hadn't expected to ask Faith to marry him, but it was right for them to be together. He was serious about eloping. He wanted to hurry and get to the forever part.

As he was walking down the hall, he got a fantastic idea. He would let the whole school know he was serious about marrying Faith. She usually didn't like making a spectacle of herself, except on stage. But this would be different. He just needed to wait till school was getting out. That would be his chance to make it official.

After the last bell rang, all the kids started pouring out of the classrooms and flooding the halls. This would be the perfect chance. He stood in his place, watching the kids passing him with smiles and goodbyes. He had a goodbye ritual with many of the students. He gave countless fist bumps and high fives. One girl pulled on his sleeve, wanting her goodbye. He gave her a fist bump and tried to keep an eye out for Faith. She was coming. He waited, and then she came through, close enough.

Ryan grabbed her wrist. She turned to him. Her class stopped behind her in two crooked lines. He pulled Faith into his arms. She looked up into his eyes, which were focused on her like laser beams. He leaned his brown head down and then quickly touched his lips to hers. Ryan was keeping her tightly in his arms.

Had her lips always been this soft? He felt her arms tighten like a vice-like grip around his shoulders, making his heart speed up. He was trying to keep a clear head, but it was hard to maintain focus when kissing her. Ryan had to admit that he liked that feeling. He heard some catcalls, cheers, and laughter. He took a quick moment and ended his gentle kiss.

He looked behind her and saw her students laughing. Faith shook herself as if trying to regain her composure.

"EW! You were kissing!" giggled Samantha.

"Is she your dirlfriend?" asked little Tollion, "Dat's dross!"

"You are not supposed to kiss people in school. You should save your kisses for your Mama; that's what Miss Rogers told me." Brianna was directly using Faith's words against her.

"Dr. Abernathy is going to give y'all after-school detention. That's just wrong," Rodney said.

Faith was stammering as she tried to answer the kids from her class. He rushed in to save the moment.

"Now, kids, I don't know if Miss Rogers wants a husband..." Ryan told the Pre-K class, still staring with big, wide eyes. "But I want a wife. Do you think I should ask her to marry me?" he asked with a wink.

"That's yucky," Amarie told him.

"Miss Rogers is a princess, so if you want to marry her, you need to be a prince," Damiana told him, starry-eyed.

"A prince?" his eyes twinkled when he looked at Faith, "I don't know if I qualify; that's a pretty tall order."

"But you are a prince, Officer Madsen. You are brave and kind; you have a smiley face, and you are handsome." the little girl said, "Isn't that right, Miss Rogers?"

"Well, Miss Rogers?" Ryan asked as he got down on one knee, "Faith Marie Rogers, will you marry me?" his eyes were blazing with love as he asked his question.

Faith stammered and couldn't make a sound. She took a deep breath.

"Of course I will!"

"I just wanted to make it official. I didn't want you trying to get out of it." he stood and whispered in her ear.

"I would never. I can't believe God is giving you to me. It's too good to be true."

He kept holding her hand. She was breathing faster, and her smile was angelic. Suddenly, she looked at the ring of children around them.

"Gracious! Kids! We're going to be late!" she almost squealed, "Come on. Your rides are waiting for you." She was still blushing bright pink as she led her class outside, "Okay, Sweeties, remember, don't leave without telling me goodbye!"

"Miss Rogers? Can I be in your wedding?" asked Damiana. "I've always wanted to be in a princess wedding. You'll be just like Belle; Officer Madsen can be the Beast, except more handsome."

"Damiana, we'll have a wedding party in our class after I marry Officer Madsen. We'll all dress up for it."

"Yay! I love you and Officer Madsen. You're my favorites."

As Faith and her class left the building, he started laughing. This had to be his best day ever. He hadn't expected it to happen this way; he'd always thought he would have planned it out in advance. This just felt so right. He knew that he was following the Spirit's lead. He knew that God had made them for each other. Now, he just needed to keep her safe.

He was disappointed that Faith wanted to stay alone, but he understood. It must be wearying not being able to stay in your own home. He wanted his home to be her home, but that would have to wait.

He wanted to elope but realized she might want a big wedding with all the frills. He didn't want to take that from her. He could be patient.

At least she had agreed to connecting rooms tonight; his priority was to keep her safe. If Charles got to her, there would be no wedding. That was a sobering thought. He forced his mind to happier channels, picturing Faith's smile when he had asked her again in the hall, in front of her class. He would do anything for her smile. He vowed he would keep her safe.

He couldn't breathe. He'd kept his cool while Ashley told him the horrible news. It had taken every ounce of self-control to keep air going in and out of his lungs. He couldn't believe what he was hearing. Faith was engaged to the policeman. For the first time, he thought that maybe she didn't love him. She knew he was here. He'd reached out to her, and now she was betraying him.

His heart was hammering. His head was pounding. His hands were trembling with rage. He was in his car, driving to Faith's apartment. He was going to take her with him. The policeman wouldn't have her; she belonged to him.

He got to her apartment and hammered on the door. He broke the front window and crawled inside. He searched every inch, tearing up things as he searched for her or some clue as to her whereabouts. In her bedroom, he found that she had left her engagement ring. She hadn't taken it with her. He grabbed it off of her dresser and put it in his pocket. Tomorrow, she would wear the ring again on her precious finger. He wouldn't take no for an answer.

He couldn't find anything to lead to her whereabouts. He climbed out the window and back to his car.

He started driving to the old woman's house; maybe Faith was there. The whole place was cordoned off when he arrived with police crime scene tape. She wasn't here. He decided to go to the policeman's house and found it today. He got there, and he could see that no one was home. He needed to be more careful. He was sure that the policeman would have an alarm system. He crept toward the house and peeked into the darkened front window. The room was dark and unoccupied. Faith wasn't here.

He was losing her. He felt his grip on his self-control slipping. He needed Faith; she was as essential to him as oxygen. He had been without her for too long; nothing felt real without her in his life. He heard his own anguished cry in his ears.

He had to find her and bring her back to him. Certainly, if he could take her back with him, he could wipe Ryan out of her mind and heart. He had to work fast. He needed to take her from Ryan as soon as possible.

He needed a new plan. He drove back to Ashely's place. As he drove, he planned. There was one place where he knew she would be. He would have to be bold. The plan was risky. There was the policeman to contend with, and he would be trouble. Everything would have to go perfectly. He would need Ashley's help.

When he returned to Ashley's, he was calm and completely controlled. He knew what he had to do. He implied that he was planning a romantic surprise for her. She would never know what was coming.

Tomorrow, Faith would be his or no one else's.

Chapter 26

After school, Ryan took Faith with him and stopped at his house to get an overnight bag. He grabbed her bags as well. Before he left, he double-checked the alarm system. When he was sure everything was secure, he returned to the truck.

"Faith, I've got our things."

"Thank you."

"Next on the agenda is getting you a ring."

"I'm so excited."

"Before we go to the jewelry store, I need to stop at the bank," Ryan told Faith as they drove in his truck.

"I don't expect a ring so expensive you need to go to the bank. I don't need anything expensive."

"I need to open my safe deposit box. I've got some things I need to get. Come with me. It shouldn't take long. I haven't heard from Doyle about how long Charles will be in custody, and I'm not taking chances."

"Is there a chance he's out?"

"It's up to a judge."

"I hope he's put away for a long time."

"I do, too. Come on. I have something I want to show you."

"What?"

"It's a surprise."

"Surprises make me nervous."

"I hope you like this one. Come on," he helped her out of the truck and led her into the bank.

As they entered the bank, he took her hand. They went to see a teller and asked to access his safety deposit box. The teller took him back to the vault where the boxes were located.

When he opened the box, he revealed a random assortment of coins, jewelry, and two ring boxes. He pulled out one of the ring boxes.

"Open it."

Faith opened it and saw a wedding set. It was two white gold bands with a white gold solitaire diamond ring between them to make one ring.

"It's beautiful."

"It was my mother's wedding set. I would love you to have it unless you want something new."

"I'm speechless."

"We'll have to get it sized to fit you. If you want it."

"I love it. It's perfect."

He took it out of the box and slipped it on her finger.

"It fits."

"I hoped it would."

"Ryan, thank you. I love it."

"If you want something else, let me know. I want you to be happy with it."

"This is wonderful. I love that it was your mother's."

"Now it's official, I've put a ring on it," he laughed, then pulled her hand to his lips, and kissed her finger where the ring sat.

"We need a ring for you, and then we'll be set."

"I was going to use this one," he opened the second ring box; it held a white gold men's wedding band.

"I like it."

"It was my dad's."

"It's perfect and a beautiful way to honor your parents."

"I'm glad you think so."

He closed the safe deposit box and put it back. Then he took Faith's hand, and they returned to his truck. He opened the door for her, and she climbed into it.

"Have you thought any more about eloping with me?" he asked as he pulled out of the parking lot.

"I have been thinking about it all day."

"Have you decided?"

"I like the idea. I have some things I want. Conditions."

"Like what?"

"First, I have to tell my parents. I just told them I got engaged. They were excited for me, for us. I don't know how they'll feel if I elope with you."

"What else?"

"I want a wedding dress."

"That's doable," he said as he drove to their hotel.

"We have to have a preacher."

"We can talk to our pastor. Anything else?"

"It has to be on the weekend."

"All of these things can be done. So, what do you say? Friday?"

"Friday? We have school."

"After school, we'll have the whole weekend to ourselves."

"Yes. That sounds like a plan."

"Great! So, let's start working on your list. Call your parents."

"I will when we get to the hotel."

"You'll be Mrs. Madsen in two days."

"We've got so much to do!"

"After check-in, we can call the church and talk to the preacher. Tomorrow, we can go straight after school to the courthouse and get a license."

"I need to talk to Evon and Ellie about helping me find a dress. Where will we get married?"

"We can ask the pastor if using the chapel is okay. I bet your parents can get here in time. We'll have Maggie, Doyle, Ellie, and Evon, too."

"You have the best ideas of anyone I know."

"Thank you."

They arrived at their hotel. Ryan parked his truck and helped Faith with her bags. They got their adjoining rooms. Ryan knocked at the connecting door.

"Knock, knock! Leave the door unlocked. I want to be able to get in if you're in danger."

"Okay, I have to call my parents first thing, especially if we're getting married on Friday."

"I'll give you some privacy. If you need me, call out."

"I will, thank you."

He was uneasy leaving her, but she needed privacy, and he would respect that. He decided to call Maggie and tell her about their plan.

"Hello, Maggie?"

"Ryan, I am so happy for you. Faith is a wonderful woman and perfect for you."

"Thank you. I have more news. Good news."

"Tell me."

"We're getting married on Friday, kind of eloping."

"That's quick."

"We're going to have people come. I want you to come. You're the closest person to my parent, and I want you to be there."

"I wouldn't miss it. But why the rush?"

"The sooner we're married, the sooner I can have her with me. I also want to keep her safe."

"Is Charles out?"

"I don't know. I haven't heard anything from Doyle."

"Is Faith going to be happy without a big wedding?"

"She's agreed to my plan."

"Maybe we can have a big reception later."

"That's a great idea. She'll love that."

Ryan's phone buzzed to let him know he had another call. He saw it was Doyle calling.

"Maggie, I'll call you back; Doyle is on the other line."

"Okay, Bye."

Ryan switched over to Doyle.

"Doyle?"

"I've got some bad news."

"Is it Charles?"

"They let him go earlier today. Not even a slap on the wrist. Your sergeant had to work hard to get you out of trouble."

"What did I do?" Ryan started pacing around the room.

"Charles said you were persecuting him because of Faith."

"What about all she told us about him."

"I know. It was horrible. This guy is wealthy and connected. Tread carefully."

"How am I supposed to keep her safe?"

"He'll get sloppy; he'll make a mistake."

"She's staying at a hotel tonight; I'm in the room next to her."

"That's good. She shouldn't be alone."

"Well, there's some good news about that. We're engaged."

"Congratulations!"

"She's agreed to marry me on Friday. We're working out the details."

"That's quick."

"I love her and want to keep her safe."

"You're good for each other."

"When we work out the details, I want you there to stand up with me."

"I'd be honored."

"We want Ellie to be there too."

"She wouldn't miss it."

"Faith's going to take this news hard. She was just starting to feel safe."

"You're there. I'm sure that Charles can't find you tonight. You should be good."

"I'll keep her safe," he vowed.

"I know you will. Good luck."

"Thanks."

Ryan ended the call. He had to tell Faith. She would be so upset. He dreaded seeing the look in her eyes when she realized Charles was free.

He summoned his courage and knocked on the connecting door.

"Knock knock!"

"Ryan?"

"We need to talk."

She opened the door apprehensively.

"Is everything okay?"

"Charles is out."

"I knew it was too good to be true. I'll never be free."

"You've got me. We're going to be together. This doesn't change our plans."

"How did he get out?"

"Apparently, he's got lots of money and good lawyers."

"I should have known," tears filled her eyes, "It will never end."

"It will. We're going to face it together."

"You mean, you still want to marry me?"

He reached for her and pulled her into his embrace.

"Friday can't come soon enough for me. This changes nothing. I love you."

"I love you too."

"Now let's get our plan for tomorrow worked out," he said as he pulled the only chair in the room up to the bed, where she went and sat down, and they discussed their plans for the upcoming day.

He sat in his rented car across the street from Lydon B. Johnson Elementary School, sharpening his knife. He was looking at the side door. Ashley would prop open that door to go to her car. Once his knives were sharpened, he called Ashley.

She picked up on the first ring.

"Charlie?"

"I've got a surprise for you."

"Bring it to the office, and I'll pick it up."

"You know how difficult that will be with Ryan on duty. He'd never let me in. He's so protective of that liar, Faith. They've made it hard for me to see you at school."

"Well, could you have it delivered?"

"No, I want to give it to you in person. I have a question I need you to answer, and I want to see you alone. I love you so much and can't wait another minute."

"It's almost my planning time. I'll come out then."

"I'll be in the side parking lot. It's better if Ryan doesn't see us until I've asked my question."

"Okay, I'll come out the side door."

"Make sure to prop it open so you can get back in. It might look bad for you if they know you're coming out of that door; I'd hate to be the reason you get in trouble."

"You're so sweet and thoughtful."

"I'll see you soon, Love."

He waited for ten minutes, reviewing his plan. It was daring, and he would need a little luck, but he had to get the love of his life back. He hid behind the passenger side of his rented grey Toyota sedan. Nothing would stop him.

He saw Ashley come out the side door and prop it open. Now was his chance. He crouched down out of sight as she walked towards her car.

"Charlie? Are you out here?" she called.

"I don't have long, Charlie. Where are you? Is this part of the surprise?"

She turned a one-eighty, put her hands on her hips, and then looked toward the building.

"Charlie? This isn't funny."

She started walking back to the school.

He crept up behind her. He grabbed her. She cried out, "Charlie? I don't like this."

She struggled to get away, but he was stronger. He wrapped her in a sleeper hold until she passed out. He was careful that she only went unconscious; he didn't need a body to explain away. He carried her to the trunk of his rental car and tied her hands and feet with a nylon cord. Then he shut the hatch. She couldn't get out. He would dump Ashley somewhere after he took Faith with him. He wasn't taking any chances. He had to hurry; someone might close the door she had propped open any minute. Then he grabbed his hunting knife from its sheath and entered the building.

Chapter 27

As Faith and Ryan walked into the school, Maggie stopped them.

"Faith, I have to see the ring!"

"It was Ryan's mom's ring," she said, holding her left hand for the older woman to see.

"Deborah would be so happy to see it on your finger. She would love you and be so glad that Ryan found you. You are good for each other. I've never seen him happier."

"Never been happier," he hugged Faith, "I've got to check in at the office; I'll see you soon. I'm keeping an eye on you."

She watched him as he walked away with a thrill of pride that he had chosen her to be his wife. He was such a wonderful man. He was strong in body, mind, heart, and faith. Ryan was everything she'd dreamed of. She had been a fool to give so much of herself to Charles.

"Ryan said you're going to get married on Friday. Are you happy with that? Do you want a big wedding? If you do speak up, Ryan can wait. Now that you said yes, he'd wait for you for as long as it took."

"I used to want a big, fancy wedding. But Charles ruined that for me. When I was engaged to him, he wanted a big production. It all had to be his way; he even picked out my dress. I hated it. It was so revealing and tight. I want something simple and modest."

"Are you going to be able to find what you're looking for on such short notice?"

"As long as it's not too revealing and I don't look like a wedding cake, I'll be happy."

"I'm sure you'll find something perfect."

"Do you think it's a mistake to get married so quickly?"

"I think you and Ryan know each other well enough. Just remember that it's not all sunshine and roses. Marriage is hard work."

"I know, that's what my mom told me. She is happy for me; she thinks the sooner I get married to Ryan, the sooner she won't have to worry as much. My parents are glad that Ryan is always looking out for me. She likes that Ryan keeps me safe."

"I've not seen him this happy in a long time."

"I've not been this happy in a long time either."

"He was a different man after Deborah died. He'd lost his way; he changed when he found you. You helped him find his way back."

"He helped me too. I never thought I'd ever trust anyone again. I think God sent Ryan to me. He is a gift from God. I'm so thankful for him."

"God knows what we need and supplies it. He knew you two needed each other. Hold onto that. I know you two will have a good marriage."

"Thanks, Maggie. I've got to prepare for the kids; there will be so much to do today."

"I'll see you later,"

Faith went to her classroom to get ready to start her day.

She went through her morning in a joyful mood. She felt so happy that nothing was getting her down. She tried to focus on the letters and numbers she was teaching, but her heart would thrill with happiness whenever she saw her left hand and the ring on her finger. She felt like singing all morning, and the kids enjoyed singing with her. All the kids were delightful, and not even the misbehavers could bring her down. She felt joyful as her planning period neared and the chance to see Ryan. Her heart praised God all morning. She even felt free from the ever-present fear of Charles.

As the morning went on toward her planning time, she grew more excited. During circle time, Damiana asked to go to the bathroom. She smiled and told the child to go. Faith looked down the hallway; no one was in there. Suddenly, she felt an unsettling feeling of unease. She looked down the hall again. It was still clear. She shook herself and closed the door.

Faith continued circle time and sat down to read to the class. She was in the middle of the story about a naughty pigeon when she heard a knock at the door. Since they were practicing good manners, one of the students, a boy named Rodney, went to the door to greet the visitor or to let Damiana back in. When the student opened the door, he screamed.

"Miss Rogers! Help!"

Her adrenaline spiked. Something was wrong. She jumped up from her chair and quickly headed to the door. What she saw made the blood freeze in her veins. It was her worst nightmare standing in front of her.

Charles was holding Damiana and had a large knife at the girl's throat, kicking Rodney away from him hard, and the boy was on the floor, holding himself and crying. The girl had started wailing.

"Hello, my Love, see what I found? You don't have all your little lambs accounted for. I found this one wandering the hallway."

"Charles?" She screamed while pulling Rodney away from him, "Evon, call 911 and the office,"

"I'll slit her throat if you do!"

"Evon, listen to him. He'll do it."

"Miss Rogers? I'm scared!" cried Damiana.

"Shut up, brat!" Charles growled and shook her.

"Give her to me, Charles. You don't want to hurt a child."

"Come with me now, Faith."

At that moment, Mandee opened her door to see the commotion.

When the door opened, Charles turned his head to the sound.

"Come out of the room, close the door, and stay put, or I'll kill her."

"He's serious! He will do it."

Mandee shut her door and entered the hallway; she called to her kids in the classroom, "Stay in the room, and don't come out."

Damiana started struggling and kept crying.

"Faith, shut this brat up, or I will."

"You're scaring her," she looked at the little girl and saw her big dark eyes wide with terror. "Damiana, I need you to be brave and stop crying."

The child was trying to stop her terrified sobs, "Miss Rogers, please help me."

"Of course. The bad man is going to let you come to me. Besides, we're reading your favorite book!" she said, trying to calm the child.

"Miss Rogers, come get me!"

"I'm going to get you, Damiana. I won't let the bad man hurt you."

"He's hurting' my neck!" Damiana was crying.

"Talk to *me*! Not that brat! I will not hesitate to kill this child if you don't talk to *me*!"

He pressed the knife onto the kid's neck, and Damiana screamed. Faith saw that she needed to continue with caution; the little girl's life depended on it.

"Of course, I'll talk to you, Charles. Tell me what you want, but please let Damiana go. You want to talk to me; leave her alone."

"If you want this kid to live, you'll come with me now."

"Of course, whatever you say. Just put her down and let her go to Ms. Davenport. Then I'll go with you."

"No deal, I won't let the kid go till I've got you."

"I'll come with you; please let Damiana go."

"It's time to come home, Faith. You've been gone too long. I've missed you, why did you leave me? I love you."

"I know you love me, Charles. I've missed you too," she was trying to appease him.

"Come on, Faith, just come back home with me, and I'll let the girl go; you don't want me to kill this little *angel,* do you?"

"No! Charles, please don't hurt her. Let her go, please. She's not who you're upset with. I'm sorry I hurt you. Just let her go. Please?"

"I told you, come with me, and I'll let the kid go. Then we can talk all about who's hurting who."

"Of course, we can talk, then I'll go with you. Just let Damiana go first."

"Come over to me, Faith! I'll put the little brat down when I have you safe in my arms."

"I'm coming, Charles. I'll do whatever you want- please let Damiana go."

"I'm afraid I can't trust you, Faith. The brat stays with me until I have hold of you. I won't let the kid go till you are with me again."

"Let her go to Ms. Davenport. I'll go wherever you want me to. I promise."

"I'm not letting her go till I have my arm around you again." He pressed his knife harder into the child's neck, and she screamed.

"Charles let her go. I'm coming to you; she's terrified; she can't hurt you. She's just a child."

"Faith, I promised I would put her down as soon as you are back in my arms, where you belong."

"Yes, I'm coming to you."

"Promise me you'll stay with me."

"Yes,"

"Stay with me forever."

"Forever," she agreed, inching toward him, her arms outstretched to take the little girl away from the madman.

As soon as Faith was within reach, Charles reached out his knife hand and encircled her with his arm, never letting go of the knife. Then he dropped Damiana, and she fell to the ground. He wrapped his arms tight around Faith. Mandee started to run to her, but Charles hissed, "Don't move, or I will kill you both."

Mandee froze. Damiana wailed.

He kissed Faith. She felt the bile rising in her throat and squirmed in his grip.

"Now you're coming with me." He started dragging her to the door.

"Let her go!" came a steely voice.

Then she saw Ryan, and her heart left her throat. Ryan would keep Damiana and Mandee safe. When she looked at his face, it was grave; the usual easy-going look in his eyes was gone. He looked fierce, like a guardian angel. She focused back on Charles, but now she wasn't afraid.

Chapter 28

Ryan walked on cloud nine as he left Faith chatting excitedly with Maggie. He smiled as he thought about Faith and their engagement. They would be man and wife on Friday. The thought filled him with joy. He sent a prayer of thanksgiving as he thought about their bright future.

A nasty thought intruded on his happiness. Charles was still free and was actively hunting for Faith. He needed to be vigilant. He took his post at the front door.

As he paced in front of the door, he saw the last person he wanted to see. Ashley was purposefully striding towards him. He inwardly groaned.

"Ryan, Charlie is free. I wanted you to know. Your vendetta against him needs to stop."

"I don't have a vendetta against him. He is the one with the problem. He's obsessed with Faith. My fiancée. I just want to keep her safe."

"He loves me! Faith is the one obsessed. She loves him, not you. That's not his fault. You need to see her for who she is and get out. Then leave Charlie alone."

"I know who she is. I know who he is. I know who you are. I want you to be safe," he said.

"Like you even care."

"I do care about you, Ashley. I want the best for you."

"You only care about yourself."

"Be careful. I'd hate to see you get hurt."

"I could say the same to you, but I don't care about you anymore." Ashley tossed her head, turned, and went down the hall to her classroom.

As the morning went on, he became impatient for his lunch break. It was still an hour away. It was only nine o'clock. He wanted to see Faith. He wanted to talk about their plans. They had so much to get done. He started making a mental list of things to get done today. The first thing they needed was to get the license. The pastor had been out of the church last night. He needed to call him to see if he could marry them on Friday and if they could use the chapel. He knew she wanted a dress, so he supposed he should find a suit. He also wanted to get her a bouquet. That would be a great surprise for her. He loved being the reason for her beautiful smile.

Suddenly, he felt uneasy in his spirit. He knew something was wrong but wasn't sure what or where the problem was. He went to the office to see the cameras. One of the parking lot cameras was all static. The camera in Faith's hallway was static as well.

"Ms. Brown, reboot cameras one and three. We need them back online ASAP."

The feeling of pervasive danger engulfed him. Something was wrong. Faith. He had to make sure she was safe. He hurried down the hall and around the corner. Something he could not define was urging him onward. All he knew was that he had to get to her classroom. "He heard a voice tell him, "Run," and he ran down the hallway. Then he heard crying from Faith's hallway. He broke into a sprint.

He stopped at the hallway door. His stomach dropped. He saw Charles holding Faith tight to himself, with a long knife at her throat. The madman was dragging her down the hall toward the outside door. He quickly took in the scene. Mandee Davenport was at her door, frozen; Damiana was whimpering on the floor.

"Let her go!" his voice commanded as he drew his gun.

Charles turned towards him, keeping hold of Faith with his knife at her throat.

"Never."

He didn't have a clean shot. Charles was positioning Faith like a shield in front of him.

"Ryan!" Faith called, "Help Damiana, see if she's hurt."

"Stop worrying about that brat. You're coming with me," Charles growled.

"Of course, Charles. I'm going with you."

Ryan walked over to the child on the floor and picked her up. It was hard not to follow Faith immediately, but the little girl was his priority.

"Damiana? Are you okay?"

"Officer Madsen, that bad man was hurting me,"

"You're safe now," he turned to the other teacher.

"Are you okay, Mandee?"

Ms. Davenport nodded and cautiously walked over to him and the little girl.

"He's getting away with Faith!" she urgently whispered.

"I'll get her back. Go to the office; I'll call the station and get back up."

He handed Damiana to the teacher, who took the little girl and ran to the office. Then, he followed behind Charles and Faith. He radioed into the station, calling for backup. They were almost to the outside door.

"I said let her go." He pulled his gun again, still trying to find a shot.

"She is mine."

"It's okay, Ryan. I'm going with him. I need you to make sure the others are all right."

"I won't let him take you."

"Tell the officer that you want to go with me. He can't stop you."

"I'm going with Charles."

"No!"

"You can't stop us. We're going out that door. She's made her choice."

"Let her go!" He couldn't get a good shot; he didn't want to miss and hit her.

The intercom beeped three times, and a panicked voice said, "Eagles to the nest!"

Charles looked around. No one was in the hallway except the three of them.

"Tell him you won't marry him." He said and looked at the ring on her finger. He pulled it off and threw it at Ryan. Then he took her old ring off its chain and roughly shoved it onto her third finger on her left hand so hard that it snapped.

She screamed in pain.

"Tell him, or he dies," he dug his knife into her neck.

"I- I- I w-won't..." she stammered.

"Faith. It will be all right; I won't let him take you."

"I won't let him hurt them or you."

She looked down the hall, then Ryan reassured her, "They're safe. You don't have to go with him. I'm not afraid of him," the words came to him from deep inside his mind, "I dwell in the shadow of the Most High, and so do you."

"Charles, let me go!" She started straining against him, fighting again.

"But you're mine. You belong to me. I love you."

"No, I don't belong to you," she struggled.

"But you love me."

"I don't love you."

When she spoke those words, in a swift movement, Charles stabbed her deep in her abdomen as he shouted in anguish, "Yes you do! You are mine!" and she screamed as she dropped like a sack of potatoes.

After he stabbed her, she fell to the floor, and he screamed incoherently.

Ryan took the shot and hit him in the gut. Charles staggered back, then dropped, and screamed, "Faith! You still love me!" Then, he began to cry and rave unintelligibly.

Ryan radioed for ambulances as he ran to her side.

"Faith! You're going to be okay. An ambulance is on the way," he said, quickly assessing the damage.

Tears trailed down her cheeks, "Ryan, is he?"

"No, he's alive, but he can't hurt you."

"Are Damiana and Mandee…"

"They're safe. You saved them," he shoved her hands onto her abdomen, pressing hard, "This will hurt."

She winced.

"Keep pressure on that. I have to check on him; I'll be right back."

He went to where Charles lay on the ground, howling in pain.

"Don't leave me!" Charles cried, "Let me die with you!"

Charles still gripped the hunting knife and slashed at himself and then at Ryan. The blade connected with Ryan's leg, cutting through his skin. Ryan kicked his knife hand, making him let go, and then he took the knife from him. He put the knife out of reach. Charles began screaming for Faith, quickly running out of breath.

Ryan took Charles' hands and applied pressure to his wound.

"Put more pressure on that."

"You. You took her from me. She is mine."

"She doesn't belong to you. You can't keep us apart."

"Ryan!"

He came back to the floor where Faith was trying to sit up.

"Take it easy. Let me help you." He said and began applying pressure to her belly.

"That hurts."

"I'm sorry, but we've got to slow the bleeding. You're going to be okay," he was trying to reassure her and himself. He started praying silently, asking God to save her life. He needed her to stay with him. "Stay with me. Paramedics will be here soon."

"My ring! My finger! Take this off," she said, looking at her hand and the showy golden ring on her broken finger.

"I had to do it. You put his ring on your precious little finger," Charles rambled.

"I think your finger is broken. They'll have to cut this ring off. I'll find your ring, but right now, focus on slowing the bleeding," he pressed hard on her other hand.

"Ryan, I'm so cold."

"I think you're going into shock. I'm here. Stay with me."

"I'm dizzy. I can't sit up."

"I've got you," he scooped her into his arms and helped apply pressure to her belly, "The ambulance is on the way. Hang on!"

"Is Charles?"

"He's alive. The paramedics will help him. You are my priority."

"Did he hurt anyone else?"

"Dr. Abernathy is calling to check on the rest of the classrooms. Stop worrying. Just focus on staying with me."

"You're pushing in too hard; it hurts."

"I've got to stop the bleeding."

"I think I'm going to pass out."

"Stay with me. Just hang on a little longer,"

"I… love… yo-," she said as her eyes closed.

He held her, trying to stop the bleeding. She looked so white and frail, and there was so much blood. He couldn't lose her. Time seemed to tick so slowly. He was afraid EMS wouldn't arrive in time to save her. He started praying out loud.

"God, help Faith. Keep her going. Don't take her away from me, please. Help her hold on. Please, let her live."

"Faith…" gasped Charles, "Don't… go…."

"If she dies, you'll have killed her."

"I… love… her! Let… me… die… too!" He labored for every breath.

Suddenly, chaos erupted. There were paramedics and police officers everywhere. An unfamiliar paramedic came to where he sat, holding pressure on Faith's belly.

"He stabbed her. I think she's in shock. I'm afraid she passed out. Her finger is broken, too."

"I've got her."

He went over to the paramedic who was treating Charles.

"He stabbed her, and I shot him. I've checked on him. He's alive. I can hear him breathing."

"What went down," a police officer asked him.

"That man is Charles Meredith. He's been stalking Faith, Miss Rogers, for a long time. I don't exactly know how he got in. He didn't come in the front door. When I came to check things out, I saw him holding her with a knife to her throat. One of the kids was on the floor crying, and another teacher was a witness. I don't know if she saw the shooting, but she knows what happened before I arrived. He stabbed Faith, and I shot him. He was insane and raving."

"Who are the witnesses," the officer asked.

"Faith Rogers, Mandee Davenport, and one of the kids, Damiana- I don't know her last name. Dr. Abernathy is checking on the rest of the classrooms. They went into lockdown." Ryan was straightforward and businesslike. He had to keep to the facts.

He saw them putting Faith on the gurney, and they began wheeling her to the ambulance. His heart was in his throat.

"I have to go with her."

"You're bleeding."

"He got me when I got the knife from him. It's over by the wall."

"I have to go with her. We're getting married."

"We have a lot of questions for you."

"I need to be with her. She might wake up and be alone. I have to know that she's okay."

"You'll get to go to the hospital after we're done here. Now go get the paramedics to look at your leg."

"Is Detective Doyle Foster here?"

"He's on his way."

"I need to speak to him as soon as he arrives."

"Good; he'll need to speak with you as well."

While the paramedics were caring for his leg, he saw them wheeling Charles to an ambulance, calling for Faith and crying. As he watched them take the evil man to the ambulance, his face grim and professional, his friend appeared.

"I talked to Dr. Abernathy. He said that Ashley Sheridan was missing. They're searching for her. Do you think Charles hurt her?"

"I don't know. I saw her this morning. We had an unpleasant encounter. Of course, all of our encounters are unpleasant."

"What happened?"

"She was angry with me, but she usually is."

"What about?"

"She isn't happy with my engagement to Faith."

"Doyle, Charles stabbed Faith. It's touch and go. Before the paramedics came, she passed out; she lost a lot of blood. I don't want to lose her."

"Give it to the Lord.

"I'm trying…"

"I'm sorry, but there will be an investigation, especially after he accused you of harassing him."

"Mandee saw him threatening Damiana and Faith. She saw him holding Faith hostage. I'm the only one who saw him stab her; I don't think anyone else saw the shooting. Do you think that will be a problem?"

"Are the cameras working in this hallway?"

"They weren't when I came to check on this hallway. Ms. Brown was rebooting them when I came this way."

"Hopefully, they caught it."

"Is Damiana okay? She should know more."

"I don't know how much she'll be able to tell us. She is traumatized."

"Poor little girl. Was she hurt badly? Mandee Davenport took her and ran as soon as I got his attention. I had to focus on him. He's insane. I had to stop him. I was too late to keep Faith safe. She needed me, and I failed her."

"You saved the school. I'm sure the investigation will exonerate you."

"I need to get to the hospital. I can't let Faith be alone; she needs me, and I need to be with her."

"I'll get you there. I'm praying for her and you. Come with me; I'll get you to the hospital."

"Thank you, brother."

Chapter 29

Ryan startled awake. His left leg stung and throbbed where Charles had cut him. His shoulders and back ached from sleeping in the uncomfortable chair.

He quickly assessed his surroundings. It was a hospital room with soft, light blue walls. The TV across from the bed showed a rerun of an old sitcom with the volume low. He looked toward the bed beside him to reassure himself that she was still there.

Faith lay asleep and still on the hospital bed. Her soft brown eyes were closed, and her face was pale. Her ring finger was in a splint and wrapped. Her arm and hand were covered in tubes and wires. One of the tubes was attached to a bag of plasma, another to a pack of fluids. She looked so vulnerable. It broke his heart.

A nurse in pink scrubs came in the door. "I'm just here to do a vitals check."

"She's been sleeping for a while. Is that normal?"

"After surgery, while the anesthesia is working its way completely out of her system, she'll probably be sleeping a lot. It's normal. I also wanted to tell you that visiting time will be over in a couple of hours."

"Do I have to leave? Someone needs to be here for her. I can't let her be alone when she wakes up."

"You can stay, but we usually don't have overnight visitors in this ward. So, you'd just have to be in the chair. I don't know if I can find you a bed."

"I don't mind the chair. When can I speak to the doctor?"

"I'm afraid you can't. Confidentiality guidelines are strict."

"But I'm her fiancé."

"But if you're not in her paperwork…"

"Well, I'll get a hold of her parents. They should be here by now."

"You can't stay without the patient's consent.

"She can't give or refuse consent- she's asleep."

"Now, settle down. You're going to wake her, and she needs her sleep. As soon as her parents get here, we'll know more."

"I'm still not leaving," he set his mouth in a stubborn line.

As the nurse left the room, Ryan wondered what he would do with himself. He felt like he'd let her down. He had promised her repeatedly that he could keep her safe, that he wouldn't let Charles hurt her again, that he would protect her. He had failed. Finally, he found a woman he loved and let her down. He hadn't stopped it. She had almost bled to death, and he'd let it happen. Big tough policeman, Ryan, did not protect Faith.

As he sat watching the rise and fall of her chest as she breathed, he became aware that he wasn't alone in the room.

"Faith!" her mom, Carolyn, cried.

Ryan saw the small woman with the same brown eyes as Faith and the same dimpled mouth, but she wasn't smiling. Carolyn had tears in her eyes.

"How is she?" the tall, balding man, Luther, Faith's dad, asked.

"She's sleeping; they operated on her. She's been awake once or twice, but not for long. The nurse told me that's normal. They won't tell me anything because I'm not on her paperwork. I told them that we were engaged, but they didn't seem to care. Now that you're here, maybe we can get some answers."

"Ryan, bless you for saving her!" Carolyn hugged him.

"I didn't; he stabbed her."

"But she's still here. He didn't take her away. Who knows what would happen if he had gotten her out of the building?" Luther reassured him.

"Now that y'all are here, maybe I can get some answers."

"Why don't you get a bite to eat, and we'll stay here with her. I've got your number, and I can text you when the doctor comes," Carolyn said.

"I can't leave her."

"You need a break, and we'd like some time alone with her," she added.

"Of course," he felt dejected; he thought her parents liked him.

"Go get some coffee and then come straight back. It will do you good," she said comfortingly.

Ryan hesitated, then pulled her hand to his lips, and softly said, "I love you, Faith. I'll be right back."

As he left, all his doubts and fears came flooding in.

Why had God let it happen? God had let that madman nearly kill her. What happened to him giving his anxieties to God? Why was God letting this happen? Tears filled his eyes, and he shook his head to clear them.

He was ambushed into a big bear hug when he got to the waiting room.

"Ryan, Honey! How is Faith? How are you? Were those her parents I saw go back?"

"Whoa, slow down, Maggie. One thing at a time."

"Sorry to overwhelm you; I'm just anxious for news."

"I don't know a lot. They won't tell me anything because I'm not on her paperwork.

"Was that couple her parents?"

"Yes. They asked me to leave. I thought they liked me. Do you think that they blame me for not saving her?"

“No one thinks that. Besides, they are right; you need a break.”

“I’m afraid, Maggie. What if she…”

“She’s in God’s hands. His will be done. Trust Him. He knows what’s best for both of you. I’ve been praying.”

“Thanks, Maggie.”

“Oh, did you hear about Ashley?”

“I heard she was missing, but my mind’s only been on Faith,”

“They found her. She was tied up in the trunk of a rental car.”

“What?”

“Some officers heard screaming from the trunk of an unknown car. When they were able to open it, she was all trussed up and madder than a hornet.”

“How did that happen?”

“She was raving! It seems that Charles, she called him Charlie, had called her to come out to surprise her, but instead, he knocked her out, tied her up, and left her in the trunk. She had propped the door to the school open. That is how he got in.”

“Wow. Is she okay?”

“Physically, yes. But emotionally, she seems devastated. She’s also in big trouble at school for not following the safety procedures.”

“I am sorry for her. She’s just as much a victim of Charles as Faith is.”

Just then, Ryan’s phone buzzed with a message from Carolyn. Faith was awake, and the doctor was in.

Chapter 30

Faith felt herself floating in the ether; she heard a voice. Whose was it? She wanted to hear only one voice- a low, rich, husky drawl. Was Ryan here? Where was she? She felt woozy, and it was hard to catch her thoughts.

"Ryan?" Her voice was a whisper.

"Momma and Daddy are here. He'll be here in a minute. He's not here right now," Carolyn said.

"Mom?" she felt her eyes fill with tears.

"Yes?"

"Is Ryan coming back?"

"Yes. He didn't want to leave."

"Mom, we're supposed to get married on Friday. What day is it?"

"It's Wednesday, about eight pm."

"It's still only Wednesday?"

"You've been through a lot in just one day."

Just then, she saw Ryan walk into the room.

"Faith!" he hurried to her side, "How do you feel?"

She gave him a weak smile and reached out her hand to him.

"I'm just a little sore."

"Call and have the nurse give you something for the pain."

"Not just yet. I think it's making me woozy."

"I just want you to be comfortable."

"I know, thank you."

He took her hand and kissed it.

"Ryan, have you heard anything about Charles?"

"Doyle told me they had him in for an operation. Now he's out of surgery, and they will take him into custody when he's released from the hospital."

"He can't get here, can he?" Panic started creeping up her spine.

"Faith, two officers are with him, and he's handcuffed to the hospital bed. Besides, I'm staying with you." Ryan reassured her.

There was a knock at the door. A small, thin, young woman with long blonde hair entered the room.

"Hello. I'm Dr. Summers."

"Doctor? What exactly is going on with my daughter?" Carolyn asked.

"She was stabbed in the abdomen. There was damage to her uterus. To stop the bleeding, I had to do a hysterectomy. I was able to save her ovaries. There was damage to her intestines; I was able to fix it before she had any real leakage. We were able to clean up everything so that she wouldn't be septic. But to be safe, we're giving her some powerful IV antibiotics and keeping her here an extra day or two."

"A hysterectomy? Does that mean I won't be able to have children?"

"You won't be able to carry a child, but I did save your ovaries, so with Invitro, you could use a surrogate to have your own children. It's a bit expensive, maybe."

She felt her heart drop. There was no way that Ryan would want to marry her now. She might not be able to give him children. He deserved better; she needed to let him go. Her heart was breaking. When she heard Ryan speak, She was roused from troubling thoughts to catch the conversation again.

"So, how long will she have to stay in the hospital?"

"Probably only three more days if she doesn't develop a fever or an infection."

"And how long will she be out of commission after she gets home?"

"She'll have restrictions for at least a month, and then we'll see how she's doing."

"We are getting married on Friday," Ryan explained.

"She'll still be here on Friday."

Faith thought that was a good thing; it would give Ryan a good chance to think about it and cancel the wedding. She couldn't let him throw his life away on her. He deserved a chance to have children. He would be a great father."

Tears filled Faith's eyes and started spilling out. She'd thought God had sent Ryan to her to be her husband. It would be hard to let that dream go. Maybe she could move back in with her parents after the end of the school year. She couldn't stay in Tulsa without Ryan. It would hurt too badly.

Ryan turned toward her and squeezed her good hand. It was too much. She started sobbing. She tried to pull herself together and ask more questions of Dr. Summers, but Ryan's loving look was her undoing.

"I can come back in a few minutes if you have any more questions." Dr. Summers said.

"Thank you, Doctor," Carolyn said as the small woman left.

Faith tried to gather her courage. She would need all of it if she set Ryan free. She would need privacy.

"Mom and Dad?"

"Yes?"

"I need a minute alone with Ryan."

"Of course. Come on, Luther."

When they were alone, Ryan bent down and pressed his lips against hers.

"Don't worry about the wedding; we'll just postpone it for a day or two. You know, I've heard of some people being married in the chapel at a hospital; we can still get married on Friday if you want to."

"Ryan, I-I," she had trouble swallowing and getting the words out of her mouth, "I can't marry you."

"What?"

"I can't in good conscience marry you."

"Why?" His eyes were wide and incredulous with shock.

"Why? You heard the doctor. I can't have kids."

"No, she said it was a maybe."

"But maybe it is a big risk. You don't want to get saddled with me and then try to spend lots of money and never have a baby."

"Faith, I love you. We can cross that bridge down the road."

"No. We have to face it now. I can't marry you."

"Don't you love me?"

Now was going to be the hard part. Should she lie to him and make him believe she didn't want to spend her life with him? Or should she explain herself? Would he understand and let her go? Did she really want him to?

"It- It's more complicated than that."

"Either you love me, or you don't. It's not complicated," his voice was strained, "because I love you. I want to marry you. I want to spend my life with you."

"I love you. I love you too much to marry you and ruin your life," she looked down at the white hospital sheets to avoid his eyes.

"How could marrying you ruin my life?"

"Because of the hysterectomy. I won't be able to have children. I don't want to take that chance away from you. You will be such a great father."

"The doctor said there was a chance."

"But it's a gamble. I'm afraid you'll resent me if things go wrong. I want you to be happy. I want you to have everything," It was so hard to try and convince him, especially because she didn't want to do it.

"You are everything I want."

"But marriage is forever. What if you change your mind down the line? You would be stuck with me."

"Do you really think that little of me? Do you really think I'm that fickle? I didn't realize you had such a low opinion of me."

"I don't think that. I don't want to ruin your chances to be a dad."

"No one can guarantee the future. God doesn't promise us that life will be all happiness. There will be hard things. That's why he created marriage; he wanted us to have a helper. I know God put us together for a reason. We are meant to be a team; God put this love for you in my heart," he took her hand and caressed it.

"But you deserve better than me."

"God put us together, and God doesn't make mistakes."

"I just want you to be happy."

"Then marry me ASAP."

"But what if…"

"Don't you trust me? What I hear you saying is that you don't trust me to love you and be with you, no matter what," his voice was sharp with hurt and disappointment.

"It's not that."

"Yes, it is. You're afraid of getting hurt. You think I'll leave you if we can't have kids."

"Maybe you wouldn't, but you would resent me. You would start to hate me."

"God has put this love in my heart and will keep it there. Or is it you resent me?"

"Why would I resent you?"

"I couldn't save you. I promised to keep you safe, and then Charles hurt you anyway."

"You kept him from taking me away. If not for you, he would never have let me go."

"It comes down to two simple questions. Do you love me? And do you trust me?"

"I do love you and trust you, but…"

"If you love and trust me, there is no but."

"Let me finish. *But* can we first wait until I'm out of the hospital?"

"We can wait if you need to. I want you to be healthy and ready. Do you still want to elope?"

"I would like to follow our plan, just wait a couple of months over Christmas break. I should be able to get around great by then."

"Okay, that just gives us more time to plan our trip."

"Do you want me to get your parents back in here?"

"I suppose we should let them in on our plans."

"Of course, I'll go find Maggie and fill her in. She's been waiting."

"Ryan, I'm tired," Faith felt her face crack in a yawn.

"You should rest. I'll get your parents."

Then, in a moment, he was out the door.

Chapter 31

Faith was sitting in her hospital bed, trying to eat breakfast. She was so excited that she could barely concentrate on eating.

"You have to finish your breakfast, or they won't let you go home," Ryan reminded her.

"I'm just so excited! I can't wait to get back to my apartment. I miss it."

"Don't get too attached to it, because in December we'll get married and live at my house. I have some ideas about the house that I need your opinion on," he reached over and patted her hand.

"Okay. Sounds fun!"

There was a knock on the door.

"Come in! I'm almost finished with breakfast, I promise."

"Sorry to interrupt your meal," a timid voice came through the doorway, and then the last person Faith expected to see entered the room. "Please, I need to talk to you," Ashley Sheridan said.

She looked like a new woman. Her hair was in a short bob with golden highlights, and her brown contacts were gone, revealing her dark blue eyes. She wasn't a copy of Faith.

Ryan glared at the woman as she entered the room.

"Faith, Ryan, I know this is my fault. I shouldn't have listened to Charlie. Charles, I should say. He tricked me into leaving the door open. I thought he was… well, it's probably best that he didn't. That's how he got in. I left the door open."

"Ashley, it's not your fault; he tricked you; he is untrustworthy."

"You warned me against him, and I just resented you for it. I believed every lie. I wanted to."

"He is a master manipulator. I was under his thrall for years."

"I- I'm sorry."

"You don't have to apologize…" Faith began.

"Yes, I do. You and Ryan tried to tell me, and all I did was try and ruin your lives."

"It's okay, Ashley," Ryan said, "you didn't ruin our lives. God had a plan all along."

"I've been very jealous of you, Faith. I used to date Ryan. He broke up with me, and I had made it my goal to ruin his life ever since."

"I understand."

"And then Charlie, I mean Charles, came. I thought he loved me. I was so blind. You tried to help me, even when I was accusing you."

"I've been there. Charles is an evil man who uses people to get what he wants."

"I let him use me; even when the signs were there, I purposely ignored them," she hung her head.

"Ashley, I am sorry that my behavior caused so much heartache for you," Ryan said.

"I'm sorry that Charles used you like that, and I forgive you," Faith said.

"I just have one question."

"Yes?"

"How can you forgive me after what I've done?"

"I can forgive you because Jesus forgave me."

"I don't get it." Ashley shook her head.

"I'm a sinner, destined for Hell, but Jesus died and took my place on the cross, paid for my sins. Then He rose again."

"You, a sinner?"

"She is, and so am I," Ryan chipped in.

"You can admit you're a sinner, Ryan?"

"I know I'm a sinner. The Bible says, "All have sinned and come short of the glory of God.""

"I've heard that before."

"Jesus paid the penalty for *everyone's* sin."

"Mine?"

"Yes, He did it so that you could join Him in Heaven for eternity," Ryan said.

"John 3:16 says, "For God so loved the world, that He gave His One and only Son so that whoever believes in Him will not perish but have eternal life," Faith added.

"I've heard that before, but I guess I never really thought about it."

"Jesus died to save you," Faith explained, excited as God gave her the words to say.

"Are you saying I wouldn't go to Heaven if I were to die right now?"

"Have you asked Jesus to forgive your sins and asked Him to live in you?"

"No."

Faith took a deep breath. She didn't want to turn Ashley away with her answer, so she asked God for the words.

"The only way to Heaven is by believing in Jesus's sacrifice and asking Him to live in you."

She heard Ryan gasp quietly as she held her breath.

"How do I do that?" Ashley asked them.

"By praying and asking Him to," Ryan explained.

"I haven't prayed since I was a kid," Ashely said, looking at Ryan with tears in her eyes. "Can you help me?"

"Pray with me," they all bowed their heads, "Dear Jesus, forgive us our sins and come and give Ashley new life with you. Please come and live in us. Amen."

"Jesus," came Ashley's quiet, shaky voice, "forgive my sins and come and live in me, please."

Faith wept softly, and so did Ryan.

"I feel like I'm free," Ashley said in amazement.

"You are free in Jesus."

"I can breathe easier now. I don't feel so empty and angry."

"Jesus lives in you now." Ryan said, "Welcome to the family of God."

"You should come to church with us tomorrow!" Faith exclaimed, "I'm getting to go because I'm getting out of the hospital today. You could sit with us and Maggie."

"You want me to go?"

"Of course."

"I'd love to."

"We'll pick you up tomorrow morning at nine o'clock for Sunday School. We're going to the late service; Faith needs to rest."

"Thank you, friends," she hugged Faith and Ryan, "Oh! I nearly forgot! I found something that belongs to you. I know that Ryan has been beside himself trying to find it."

"What?"

After digging through it, Ashley got her purse, pulled out something small, and handed it to Ryan.

Ryan held it, and a smile spread across his face.

"You found it?"

"Yesterday, after school. It was under one of the lockers in the Early Childhood Hall. I saw a sparkle on the way to the teacher's lounge. At first, I thought it was a costume piece that one of the kids brought to school and lost. After I inspected it, I realized what and whose it was."

"I've been so worried that I wouldn't find it. I thought I searched everywhere."

"I wanted to give it to you myself as a gesture of good faith."

"Thank you so much!"

"Well, aren't you going to put it where it belongs?"

Ryan had an excited twinkle in his blue eyes as he took Faith's left hand.

"I think this belongs to you," he said, placing the ring in her palm.

"My ring!"

"As soon as your finger is healed, I'm putting it on your finger, and there it will stay."

He took her hand in his and kissed it.

"Thank you, Ashley!" Faith felt tears in her eyes.

"I'm glad to see it back where it's supposed to be." Ashley smiled.

"Ashley, you know that now you're a part of God's family; we're brothers and sisters in Christ. I'm so glad. I'm always here for you if you need someone to talk to about Charles and what he did to you."

"Thank you. I might take you up on that. He really messed my life up. I want to be myself again, but better. Now I am a new me, and I'm free."

"I'm so happy and excited for you."

"I feel like that anger and bitterness are gone. I truly hope the two of you will be happy."

"Thank you. We've changed our wedding date to December 20th, the day school gets out for Christmas break." Faith gushed, "I should be all healed up by then."

"I am truly happy for you. It's strange. I didn't think I would be, but now that I have Jesus, everything has changed."

"Now that you have Christ, you are a new creation; the old you is gone, and the new you has come."

"I'm actually excited to go to church with you tomorrow! I'll be ready. See you at nine!"

"Give me a hug before you go," Faith told her, "I think this is the start of a beautiful friendship," she said as she embraced Ashley.

"I don't want to keep you; it looks like you're getting ready to go."

"I get to go home when the doctor releases me this morning."

"I'm glad. I will see you both tomorrow."

"Goodbye,"

After Ashley closed the door, Ryan hurried to Faith's side, enveloping her in a bear hug.

"That was amazing," he said, "We make a great team."

"Ryan, you were magnificent! I was so proud of you. Have you ever done that before? Led someone to the Lord?"

"This was a first. I was so scared I would mess up, but God gave me peace and the words to say. It was so awesome."

"It's exciting that she got saved! Being here while it happened and helping was a first for me, too."

"We did it together with God. Maggie won't believe this!"

Then Ryan wrapped his arms around Faith and kissed the top of her head.

Epilogue

It was a mildly chilly day without a cloud in the sky, a perfect December day for a wedding. Faith arrived at the church and went into the bride's ready room; she started pouring out prayers of thanksgiving and praise as she got dressed. God had been so faithful to them. Things had worked out for them perfectly.

The video cameras in the hallway had rebooted just in time to show Charles and his knife at her throat. The testimony of Mandee Davenport had helped to exonerate Ryan of any wrongdoing in the shooting completely.

Ashley Sheridan's testimony had been the final nail in Charles Meredith's coffin. He wouldn't be getting out of prison for a long time.

With Ryan at the school and God's word in her heart, she was able to get back to a sense of safety. The first day back, she had frozen as she entered the hallway. She'd had a flash of the horror of the scene. But Ryan put his hand to her back and urged her to her classroom. "I will not let you fail." he had whispered. After a week, she was able to come and go without fear.

Damiana had been severely traumatized, but she was doing better. She never wanted to leave Faith or Ryan's sides. In fact, Faith had asked her grandmother if Damiana could be her flower girl. They hadn't wanted a big, fancy wedding, but it was helping the child deal with her ordeal.

She looked at her left hand and saw the engagement ring. It made her thankful for her growing friendship with Ashley. Ashley had been baptized and was coming to a Women's Bible Study that Maggie, Evon, Ellie, and she attended. God was blessing her in so many ways.

Her joy overflowed. Today, she and Ryan pledged their love and commitment to each other. Her impossible dream was coming true.

Faith checked herself in the mirror. Her long dark hair was swept up in front and free flowing in the back. She had a simple white dress that hung just past her knees and a pair of slim knee-length beige boots.

She smiled at her reflection. Not too fancy, just simple and elegant, perfect for the small, intimate ceremony they had planned.

Her mother came into the room.

"How are you feeling? Nervous? Excited? Happy?"

"Grateful. Ryan is the answer to prayers I was afraid to ask. I never thought I'd have a love like this. I'm so thankful to God for giving him to me."

"I'm so happy for you. Now, do you have everything you need?"

"I have my ring, which was Ryan's mom's; that's old. My dress is new. I borrowed this pearl necklace from you. I had Daddy put a penny in my shoe. Mom! I don't have something blue!"

Carolyn carefully hugged Faith so as not to muss her hair. "Calm down, Faith."

There was a knock at the door.

Maggie was at the door.

"Honey! You're so beautiful! I just had to come and give you this small gift from Ryan. It was also his mother's."

She held out a small box to her.

"Open it!" Carolyn urged.

She opened the grey velvet box. Inside was a ring of sapphires arranged in the shape of a cross.

"It's perfect! Now I have something blue!"

"Thank you for bringing this to me, Maggie. Hug me."

"I don't want to mess up your gorgeousness."

Faith shrugged her off and gave Maggie an exuberant hug.

"Thank you for taking care of Ryan until I could find him. You've kept him from going off the deep end. You kept him grounded, and his heart prepared us to find each other. I know God put you in our lives. You are like a second mom to me. Thank you for being here to share this day with us."

There was another knock on the door.

"Faith, it's time!" Evon called.

"Here I go!" Faith said, walking out the door to meet her father, who was waiting to take her to her future.

Faith followed Damiana down the aisle. She looked down at Ryan as she walked unceremoniously with Luther to the front of the chapel. His blue eyes sparkled, and his smile was enormous. His dimples were on display. He took her hand and gave it a gentle squeeze.

"You are beautiful," he whispered.

She held a simple bouquet of pansies in her hand, which she handed to Evon, who stood beside her with little Damiana.

She took Ryan's hand, and he kissed hers.

Their minister asked them age-old questions, and they solemnly gave their 'I dos.' He joyfully led them through sacred vows as they pledged their love and lives to each other.

"I now pronounce you man and wife. You may kiss the bride!"

Ryan pulled Faith to his chest and sealed their promises with a kiss. The kiss was sweet and full of love with a hint of passion underneath.

"May I present to you for the first time, Mr. And Mrs. Ryan Madsen. Congratulations, and may God bless you.

Ryan pulled her arm through his, and he kissed her cheek.

"I love you," he mouthed into her ear as they walked arm in arm, out of the chapel and into their future.

About the Author

Angie DeWoody-Mitchell attended Northeastern State University in Tahlequah, Oklahoma where she studied theater, literature, and early childhood education. She lives in Fort Gibson, OK. Angie is an actress, improv artist, and avid reader. She also teaches the first-grade Sunday School class and Kids' Worship at First Baptist Tahlequah. Angie is a Christian, wife, mother, and daughter who relies on Christ daily. As the daughter of a preacher, Angie grew up in a supportive Christian family.